LUTON LIBR

D0587165

EX LIBRIS

VINTAGE CLASSICS

9 39651391

WRECKERS MUST BREATHE

Ralph Hammond Innes was born in Horsham, Sussex, on 15 July 1913 and educated at Cranbrook School, Kent. He left school aged eighteen, and worked successively in publishing, teaching and journalism. In 1936, in need of money in order to marry, he wrote a supernatural thriller, *The Doppelganger*, which was published in 1937 as part of a two-year, four-book deal. In 1939 Innes moved to a different publisher, and began to write compulsively, continuing to publish throughout his service in the Royal Artillery during the Second World War.

Innes travelled widely to research his novels and always wrote from personal experience – his 1940s novels *The Blue Ice* and *The White South* were informed by time spent working on a whaling ship in the Antarctic, while *The Lonely Skier* came out of a post-war skiing course in the Dolomites. He was a keen and accomplished sailor, which passion inspired his 1956 bestseller *The Wreck of the Mary Deare*. The equally successful 1959 film adaptation of this novel enabled Innes to buy a large yacht, the *Mary Deare*, in which he sailed around the world for the next fifteen years, accompanied by his wife and fellow author Dorothy Lang.

Innes wrote over thirty novels, as well as several works of non-fiction and travel journalism. His thrilling stories of spies, counterfeiters, black markets and shipwreck earned him both literary acclaim and an international following, and in 1978 he was awarded a CBE. Hammond Innes died at his home in Suffolk on 10 June 1998.

HAMMOND INNES

Wreckers Must Breathe

VINTAGE BOOKS
London

Published by Vintage 2012

2 4 6 8 10 9 7 5 3 1

Copyright © The Estate of Hammond Innes 1940

This book is sold subject to the condition that it shall not,
by way of trade or otherwise, be lent, resold, hired out,
or otherwise circulated without the publisher's prior
consent in any form of binding or cover other than that
in which it is published and without a similar condition,
including this condition, being imposed on the
subsequent purchaser

First published in Great Britain by Collins in 1940

Vintage
Random House, 20 Vauxhall Bridge Road,
London SW1V 2SA

www.vintage-classics.info

Addresses for companies within The Random House Group
Limited can be found at: www.randomhouse.co.uk/offices.htm

The Random House Group Limited Reg. No. 954009

A CIP catalogue record for this book
is available from the British Library

ISBN 9780099577348

The Random House Group Limited supports the Forest Stewardship
Council® (FSC®), the leading international forest-certification organisation.
Our books carrying the FSC label are printed on FSC®-certified paper. FSC is
the only forest-certification scheme supported by the leading environmental
organisations, including Greenpeace. Our paper procurement policy can be
found at www.randomhouse.co.uk/environment

Typeset in Bembo by Palimpsest Book Production Limited,
Falkirk, Stirlingshire
Printed and bound in Great Britain by Clays Ltd, St Ives plc

To

The village of Cadgwith in Cornwall.

Where I spent my last holiday before the war and where
I hope to spend my first holiday when it is all over.

Contents

Part One

The Disappearance of Walter Craig

1

Interrupted Holiday

Cornwall is a wrecker's coast. But when I left for my holiday I thought of the wrecker as a picturesque ruffian of several centuries ago who lured ships to their destruction with false beacons and waded out into the angry seas to knife the crew and unload the cargo as the vessel broke up. I did not think of Cornwall as being still a wrecker's coast, and I knew nothing of the modern wreckers I was to find havened beneath the shadow of those grim cliffs. I had intended going to the Lakes, but fate decreed that the gathering storm of the Polish crisis should keep my companion at his desk in the newsroom and that I should pick on the Lizard for my holiday.

I stayed at Church Cove, where white, thatched cottages, massed with flowers, straggled down a valley to the dark cleft of the cove with the round capstan house on its shingle beach rotting because no boats came. The Kerris's cottage, where I stayed, was at the upper end of the village and backed on to a farm.

The cottage was really two cottages thrown into one to make a guest house. Kerris, who had done the knocking together himself, was very proud of the result. Before I had been there half an hour he was taking me over the place, showing me with his toothless mouth agrin all the pieces he had obtained from the *Clan Malcolm* which had been wrecked that winter. He had relaid the floors throughout the cottage during the winter and as far as I could gather the work had all been done with wood from the *Clan Malcolm*. There were brass doorsteps, chairs and ship's lamps, all from the same luckless ship. He was a great wrecker, was Kerris. When I expressed my amazement at the amount of stuff he had collected from that one ship, he shook his head with a rueful smile. 'Ar, she were a grand wreck,' he said. 'We'll never see the like o' her again, sir—never. She came ashore this side of the Lizard. Caught on the rocks, she was, and broke her back. She was no use for salvage purposes, so Lloyd's told the Cadgwith people that if they liked to go out and salvage what they could and put it up for auction in the village they might collect a percentage of the proceeds.' He shook his head again. 'Ar, she were a grand wreck, sir. If we had one like that every winter, we'd not have to work.'

I spent five days there in a pleasant haze of bathing, lazing, pubs and Cornish cream. Then Thursday dawned, and with it the shock of a newspaper placard at the Lizard—Soviet-German Non-Aggression Pact. I stopped the car and stared at it unbelievingly. Groups of holidaymakers stood about outside the newsagents' reading the papers and talking in low tones. Europe, Hitler, the whole world-fear of Nazism seemed suddenly to have enveloped the place like a sea mist. I jumped out of the car and bought a copy of my own paper, the *Daily Recorder*. It was true enough, and, what was more, Britain was calling up reserves and there were reports of mobilisation in France.

I tossed the paper into the back of the car and drove on to Gunwalloe Church Cove, the other side of Mullion. What was the use of spoiling a holiday by getting upset about the international situation? Wasn't this what I had expected—the usual autumn crisis? But I had not expected a Soviet-German Non-Aggression Pact and I knew that it might well throw all calculations out of gear. The fear of a war on two fronts removed, the German High Command might well decide to make a lightning thrust against Poland and then, if necessary, fight it out with the democracies on the Western Front.

I thought it all out as I drove across the Goonhilly Downs

with the warm heavy scent of sun after rain in my nostrils, and by the time I had convinced myself that the pact was not as serious as it had at first seemed, it was twelve o'clock, and I was at Gunwalloe Church Cove. Two days ago there had been at least three hundred cars in the park. I counted a bare fifty. The beach seemed empty. Yet it was a glorious day. I had a bathe and then strolled along the beach. A tubby little man in grey flannels with a panama stuck squarely on his head nodded to me. 'Things look pretty bad this morning, don't they?' he said.

'Not too good,' I replied. 'But it's a fine day.'

'Aye,' he said, 'that's raight, it is. And we'd best make the most of 'em. Two men in our hotel have been called oop. Wired for last night.'

Five minutes' conversation with this gentleman left me with a feeling of utter depression. I had lunch and tried to settle down to read, but my mind would not concentrate and I was conscious all the time of the emptiness of the beach. I had my third bathe of the day and went home to tea to find the cottage empty of visitors. The two couples had gone; one of the men was in the emergency reserve of officers and the other had received a telegram from his office.

And yet, as I had driven back, I had seen the harvest being gathered in and had passed cows being driven to the farms to be milked. It had only touched Cornwall through the visitors. It had not touched the real Cornwall. The everlasting struggle of man to extract from the soil and sea a winter's living went on just as before. That was reality. While that other life of diplomacy, propaganda, machines and herded populations tense and fearful with the sense of impending catastrophe was artificial, a complicated nightmare conjured by civilization. I sat for a while over my tea, wrapped in the horror of it. Before my mind's eye swept fragmentary pictures of the last war. I had been at school, but it had not passed me by entirely. I remembered the cadet corps, the boys who left never to return, the dark nights in London and the searchlights flickering like pencils across the sky; the troop trains and the hospital trains; Summerdown Camp, Eastbourne. And then I remembered the books and the plays that had followed—Sherriff's *Journey's End*, Remarque's *All Quiet*, now banned in Germany, and Henri Barbusse's *Under Fire*. It could not happen again. But I knew it could. A new generation and the horror is lost in the glory that is cried to the rooftops by a ruthless propaganda machine, and from the rooftops echoes back to a nation steeped in Wagnerian idolatry.

The radio interrupted my thought and the bland voice of the announcer gave me the weather forecasts. I waited, fascinated, yet wanting to get away from the damned thing and enjoy my holiday. More incidents on the Polish frontier. Berlin report of ten German soldiers shot on their own side of the frontier. Polish customs officials seized in Danzig. Mobilisation in France. More British reservists called up. I got up and went out into the quiet of the evening. The announcer's voice followed me down the street. I made for the cove and then struck away to the left towards Cadgwith.

I reached the top of the cliffs and paused for a moment to look down at the calm leaden sea that heaved gently against the rock-bound coast. The cry of the gulls was balm to the turmoil of my thoughts. That high screaming cry had always been synonymous with holidays to me, for from my earliest childhood I had always spent them on the rocky coastlands. There was peace here and quiet. I looked back at the little group of cottages huddling down the valley to the cove. It was satisfying to think that whatever happened this coast and the cottages would remain to bring peace of mind to those who lived on and to other generations. Two gannets swung effortlessly down the coast, their black wing-tips showing clearly in the slanting rays of the sun. The air was still and breathless. Not a ripple stirred the burnished surface of the sea and the white streaks of the currents setting from the Lizard were plainly visible. Every now and then a little patch of dark troubled water showed as a shoal of mackerel or pilchards broke the surface in their evening play.

I went on with the ache of a great beauty and a great peace in my heart. The other world that was mirrored like a monstrous nightmare in the pages of the newspapers seemed even more unreal. Being a dramatic critic, I think I had become infected with a characteristic which I have often noticed in actors—I was unable to apprehend reality. Probably because their brains and senses are so accustomed to reacting to stimuli which are imaginatively but not factually true, actors envisage the situation more vividly than the next man, but once envisaged, it is done with. They have difficulty in accepting it as actual, irrevocable. There is an instinctive feeling that at the appointed hour the curtain will come down and one can go home to supper. I think I suffered now from this limitation—or if you like this blessed ability. However grim the drama, I felt there must still be an alternative world outside it. Thus I alternated between moods of blank despair and moods of refreshing, almost gay normality.

Twenty minutes' walking brought me to the Devil's Frying Pan. I skirted that huge circular inlet with its archway of grass-grown rock to the sea and, passing through a farmyard, obtained my first glimpse of Cadgwith. They say it is the only real fishing village left in Cornwall. Certainly the little fleet of blue boats drawn up side by side on the beach and the wheeling screaming gulls dominate the huddle of white thatched cottages. The noise of the gulls is incessant and the boats and the smell of fish testify to the industry of the villagers. And yet the place looked sleepy.

I went down the steep road to the village itself. There were cars drawn up by the shingle. One, backed close against the lifeboat, had a string of mackerel tied to its bonnet. Opposite the cars, on an old spar which did service as a bench, fishermen were sitting, smoking. I went on to the pub. The place was dark and thick with tobacco smoke and there was the airless warmth that men love who lead an open-air life. On the wall was a painting of the village. It was by a local artist, I discovered later, but it missed something. It took me some time to realize what it was. The village dominated the boats. If I had been painting the village, I should have done it so that it reeked of fish.

I ordered a bitter and sat down next to a big man in a fisherman's jersey. He had a small beard and this increased the Slav effect of his high cheekbones and small nose. A heated discussion was in progress. I caught the word spongecakes several times. An old fisherman was thumping the table angrily, but I could make no sense of what the whole room was arguing about. I asked the man with the beard. 'Oh, they've bet him five bob he can't eat a dozen spongecakes straight off. You know, the old game—it looks easy, but after you've had about four your mouth gets so dry you can barely swallow.'

'I tell you it's easy,' the old man roared, and the whole room laughed knowingly.

At that moment a young fellow in dungarees came in. His plimsoles were sopping wet and his hair curled with salt water. He went straight over to two lads seated at a table in the corner drinking from pint glass tankards. 'What luck?' they asked.

For answer he tossed a telegram on to the table. 'I'm afraid you'll have to count me out tomorrow. I've got to join my ship at Devonport. I'm leaving right away.'

Their conversation was drowned in a sudden flood of talk. 'It's been the same hall of the bloody day,' the old man who had wanted to eat the spongecakes said. 'The visitors hare going back and some of hour lads have been called up for the naval reserve.'

'Did ye see the fleet going down the Channel?' somebody asked.

'They've been going down the whole ruddy day,' said a young round-faced man. 'I seen 'em from my boat. They bin going down all day, 'aven't they, Mr Morgan?' he asked the coastguard, who was sitting smoking quietly with his back against the bar and his white-rimmed hat on the back of his head.

He nodded. 'That's right, Jim—all day.'

'Did ye see how many there was, Joe?'

'Ar, I didn't count,' replied the coastguard, his voice quiet but firm.

War had invaded the snug friendliness of the bar. The older men began to talk of the last one. The man next to me said, 'I counted upwards of fifty. That'll fix Italy all right.'

I felt somehow annoyed that talk of war had obtruded even into the warm seclusion of this pub. 'To hell with the war,' I said. 'I'm trying to enjoy a holiday.'

'What's wrong with a war?' he demanded with a twinkle in his grey eyes. 'A war would see us nicely through the winter. It's either that or steamboating.'

I looked at him. Behind the twinkle in his eyes was a certain seriousness.

'Yes,' I said, 'it must hit you pretty bad coming two years in succession and right on the holiday season.'

'Well, it wasn't so bad last year—it came later.' There was a trace of a brogue in his voice, but otherwise it was devoid of any local accent. 'Even then,' he said, finishing his beer, 'I had to do six voyages. It'll be worse this year. You can't make enough out of fishing nowadays to carry you through the winter. And the Government doesn't give any help, sir—though they want us badly enough when it comes to war.'

'Can't you do any fishing in the winter?' I asked.

He shrugged his shoulders. 'We go out when we can, but mostly the sea is pretty big outside. And then we've got all our gear to make. We're running two hundred pots a boat here, as well as nets. And there's not so much fish as there used to be. They change their grounds. Something to do with the Gulf Stream, I suppose. I tell you, sir, this is a dying industry. There's only three thousand of us left on these coasts now.'

I said, 'Yes, I know. Down at Mullion, for instance, all the young men are going off to work in the towns.'

'Ar, but you won't find that here. We're not afraid of work. The young 'uns, they're not afraid of work either. Now, in the summer, we're out at five with the pots. And then when I come in, I'm taking parties out for the rest of the day. Sometimes I take out three parties a day. That's pretty long hours.'

I nodded and ordered two beers. He took out a pouch and rolled a cigarette. 'Have one?' he asked. We lit up and sat drinking in silence for a while. It gave me an opportunity of studying him. He was a man of tremendous physique. He was over six feet with broad shoulders and a deep chest. The beard completed the picture. With his Slav features and shock of dark brown hair he looked a real buccaneer.

His eyes met mine. 'You're thinking that all I need is the gold earrings,' he said unexpectedly.

I felt extremely awkward until I saw the twinkle in his eyes. Then I suddenly laughed. 'Well, as a matter of fact,' I said, 'that's just what I was thinking.'

'Well, you must remember that some of the Armada was wrecked on these coasts. There's Spanish blood in most of us. There's Irish too. When the fishing industry was at its height down here girls would come from Ireland to do the packing.' He turned to the bar and tossed a florin on to it. 'Two halves of six,' he ordered.

'No, I'm paying for this,' I said.

'You're not,' he replied. 'It's already ordered.'

'Think of the winter,' I said. 'I'm on holiday. It doesn't matter to me what I spend.'

He grinned. 'You're drinking with me,' he said. 'We're an independent lot of folk down here. We don't sponge on visitors if we like them. Our independence is all we've got. We each have our own boat. And though you can come out mackerel fishing with us and we'll take your money for it, we'll not take you out if we don't like you.'

'Anyway,' I said glancing at my watch, 'I ought to be starting back. I shall be late for my supper as it is. I walked over from Church Cove.'

'Church Cove,' he said, as he placed a stein of beer in front of me. 'I'll run you back in the boat.'

'That's very kind of you. But it won't take me long to walk it and you certainly don't want another trip in your boat when you've been out in it all day.'

'I would. It's a lovely evening. I'd like a quiet run along the coast. The boat's out at her moorings. It won't take me ten minutes.'

I thanked him again and drank my beer. 'Why did you call this a half of six?' I asked. 'What beer is it?'

'It's Devenish's. There are three grades—fourpence, sixpence, and eightpence a pint. If you came here in the autumn you'd only be offered four.'

I nodded. 'Do you like steamboating?'

'Oh, it's not so bad. It would be all right if I could take Cadgwith along with me. I hate leaving this place. I did six voyages to the West Indies last winter. You can always pick up a berth at Falmouth. This time I think I'll try a tanker on the Aden route. If there's a war, of course, we'll be needed for the minesweepers or on coastal patrol.'

I offered him another beer, but he refused and we left the pub. It was not until we were walking down the village street in the pale evening light that I fully realized the size of the man. He was like a great bear with his rolling gait and shaggy head, and the similarity was even more marked when he had put on his big sea boots, for they gave him an ungainly shambling walk.

I enjoyed the short run back to Church Cove. For one thing, it gave me my first glimpse of the coast from the sea. For another, I got to know my friend better, and the more I knew of him the more I liked him—and the more I was intrigued. In that short run we covered a multitude of subjects—international situation, bird life on Spitzbergen, stocks and shares, Bloomsbury, Cadgwith. My impression of him was of a rolling stone that always and inevitably returned homesick to Cadgwith. But though he had obviously gathered no moss—he lived in a little hut on the slopes above Cadgwith—he had certainly gathered a wide knowledge of life, and that knowledge showed in his eyes, which were shrewd and constantly twinkling with the humour that bubbled beneath the stolid exterior of the man. His nature was Irish and his features Slav, and the mixture was something new to me.

Once I expressed surprise, for he told me that War Loan had risen ⅞ to 89⅜ on the previous day and suggested that, since the Stock Exchange was apparently taking quite an optimistic view of the situation, war did not seem likely.

I could not help it. I said, 'What do you know of stocks and shares?'

He grinned at my surprise. 'I could tell you the prices of quite a number of the leaders,' he said. 'I always read the City page of the paper.'

'Well, it's the first time I ever heard of a fisherman reading the City page of a paper,' I said. 'Whatever do you read it for?'

'I'm in a capitalist country, running a luxury business. Stock and share prices are the barometer of my summer earnings. When prices were going up in 1935 and 1936, I did pretty well. Since then there's been a slump and I have to go steamboating in the winter.' He looked at me with that twinkle in his eyes. 'I read a lot of things you probably wouldn't expect a fisherman to read. There's a free library over to Lizard Town. You can even get plays there. I used to be very fond of plays when I was in London.'

I explained that plays were my life and asked him what he had done in London. 'I was in a shipping office for a time,' he said. 'But I soon got bored with that and turned to stevedoring. I was with the River Police for a time. You know, you meet people down here, quite important people, on holiday. And they say you're wasting your time in Cadgwith. It's not difficult to get the offer of a job in London or to pull strings when you're there. But London is no life for a man. After a few months, Cadgwith calls to me again, and I come back.'

That I suppose was why he spoke so well. Talking to me, his voice had no trace of the sluggish Cornwall accent. Yet I had noticed that the local accent came readily enough to his lips when he spoke to the villagers.

Interspersed with our conversation, he pointed out interesting parts of the coastline as we went along. He showed me the seaward entrance to the Devil's Frying Pan with its magnificent arch of rock. He also pointed out Dollar Ogo to me. The cave did not look particularly impressive from the outside, but he told me that students from the 'varsity had come down and explored it for five hundred yards. 'They had to swim most of the way,' he said, 'pushing biscuit tins with lighted candles in front of them.'

'How far can you get up it by boat?' I asked. I was thinking that it would give me such an excellent opportunity of examining the various rock formations. Geology was one of my hobbies. But his reply was, 'Not very far.'

When we arrived at Church Cove, I said, 'I must come out mackerel fishing with you some time.'

'Any time you like, sir,' he said as he carried me pick-a-back ashore. 'Any of the boys will tell you where I am.'

'Who shall I ask for?' I enquired.

'Ask for Big Logan,' he replied, as he shoved the boat off and scrambled on board. 'That's what they all call me.'

'After the Logan Rock?' I asked with a grin.

He looked at me quite seriously and nodded. 'Quite right, sir,' he said. 'After the Logan Rock.'

That was the last I saw of Big Logan for a whole week. When I got back to the cottage I found a letter waiting for me. It was from my editor. He was not recalling me, but he wanted me to do a series of articles on how the international situation was affecting the country.

Kerris came in to see me after supper. He had seen that the letter was from my paper and he wanted to know whether I was leaving or not. I explained the position and said that I might be away a night or two, it depended how far afield I found it necessary to go for material. 'By the way,' I said, 'do you know Big Logan of Cadgwith?'

'Surely,' he said. 'Why?'

'He brought me back here from Cadgwith this evening by boat. Nice fellow, isn't he?'

'Ar, very nice fellow to speak to,' was his reply. 'To speak to, mind you.' He looked at me for a moment and the temptation to gossip was too much for him. 'But no good,' he said, shaking his head. 'Not worth that plate. Comes of a good family, too—his mother was a lady at one of the big houses over to Helford.'

'And his father?' I asked.

'One of the fishermen at Cadgwith.'

And then I understood why it was that he had been named Logan. It explained so much of his complex character. 'He was born at a house near the Logan Rock, wasn't he?' I asked.

'Ar, it was at the farm up there.' He shook his head. 'But he's no good,' he said. 'He's proved that. He married a Birmingham girl who was here on holiday. She had money and she built a house over to Flushing in Gillan. She were a lovely garl. But he didn't know when he was well off. He played around with the local garls and she's divorced him now and gone back to Birmingham. Now he lives alone in a little shack in Cadgwith.' He shook his head again. 'He's no good is Big Logan,' he said as he went out of the room.

I smiled to myself at that. Generations of wreckers in Kerris, I felt, spoke that condemnation of Big Logan. I felt sure that it wasn't because he had fooled around with the local girls that he thought Big Logan no good, but because, having got on to a good thing, Big Logan had let it go as Kerris never could have done. Big Logan's parentage explained so much.

That evening I settled down by the light of the oil lamp and wrote the first of my articles. The other two, however, were not so easily written and required a good deal of travelling, including an excursion into Devon, where I spent a night at Post Bridge in the midst of Dartmoor. Cornwall was much more affected by the crisis than Devon, for in general it was the departure of the visitors that brought it home to the country districts at that time. Not until later were the farmers inundated with schemes for growing more food. It is true that in the towns and even in the villages men were being called up, but this hardly touched Dartmoor and the more agricultural areas of Devon. In South Devon and in South Cornwall, however, I found the atmosphere very tense around the big towns. I had a look at Falmouth, Devonport and Plymouth, and in none of these ports was a warship to be seen. 'Most of them left last Thursday,' I was told. It was this departure of the fleet that brought it home to them. That and the appearance of sandbags, tin helmets and gas masks.

Back at the Lizard again I found things much the same. There were fewer visitors and the villagers spoke of cancelled bookings. But visitors still came and gradually everything was slipping back towards normality. Most of the tourists I spoke to were trying desperately hard to ignore the news and enjoy their holidays. 'God knows when we'll get another,' was their justification. But they read the newspapers just the same and still hoped against hope.

Then on Thursday, August 31, came the news that the children were to be evacuated and I had to re-write my final article, for Cornwall was a reception area and this brought the crisis right home to even the remoter farms and villages. On Friday I spent the day lazing and bathing, determined to forget the war scare. But when I got back I was just in time to see the first bus-load of Midlands children arrive with their teachers at Lizard Town. They looked tired, but happy. I stopped and spoke to them. They thought it a grand adventure. I found one little boy with a gas mask that seemed larger than himself who had never been outside Birmingham streets. There were many who had never seen the sea. I went home to be met by Kerris in a state of some excitement. 'Have you heard the news, Mr Craig?' he asked. 'Germany has marched into Poland. It came through on the news midday. And we've got three little boys billeted on us. Fair bastards they be. Still, mustn't grumble. Government pays us eight-and-sixpence each for them.'

My stomach felt suddenly hollow within me. So it was war after all. Somehow, I had always felt that Hitler must climb down if we called his bluff. 'Well, at least the tension is over,' I said dully. 'We know the worst.'

When I had finished my tea I went out for a walk, taking the path along the cliffs towards Cadgwith. The peace of the coast closed in around me, but it was a bitter balm. The fact that this would remain, whatever happened to my generation, no longer afforded me the satisfaction it had done a week earlier. Rather, I hated it for its aloofness and felt that it had no right to be so serene and beautiful when all Europe was to be subjected to the torture of war. I found myself even longing for the appeasement of the previous September. But it was the cry of emotion rather than reason. I knew that it could not be this time. We were not simply tied to Poland by a treaty. We were faced with the forces of oppression and brute force and we had to tread them under-foot before they ran riot over all Europe and had outgrown the strength of democracy.

I found myself suddenly looking down upon Cadgwith without any knowledge of the walk there. It was just the same as before, the boats drawn up on the beach, the gulls wheeling and screaming, the little white cottages and the smell of fish. That men were dying in a desperate fight for freedom against a mechanised army that had no thought but those instilled into its soldiers by a vast propaganda machine, left this little fishing village untouched. And the probability was that it never would be touched. I shrugged my shoulders. War or no war, there was no reason why I should not get an evening's fishing. I went down into the village and found Big Logan operating the donkey engine that hauled the boats up. While the wire hawser was being hitched on to the next boat I had time to arrange for two hours' fishing on the following day at six in the evening. I went to the pub where I heard that five destroyers had been seen going down the Channel. The rumour was that they were going to pick up the *Bremen* now two days out from New York after the hold-up by the American authorities. And I spoke to a man who said that the coastguard had seen a submarine about six miles off the coast moving westward. 'That will be a bloody U-boat,' my informant told me.

Like all the other people still on holiday, I tried hard to treat the following day as a normal one. Only when actually in the water, however, did I forget the atmosphere of tension that gripped me. On the beach, I felt moody and depressed. I could not settle down to enjoy the sunshine and the temptation to go back to the cottage to listen to the news bulletins which were broadcast with disturbing frequency was too much for me. Automatically I listened to broadcast after broadcast that were no more than a repetition of the previous ones, in most cases not even worded differently. There was nothing new—no ultimatum, no outbreak of hostilities on the Western Front; only the rapid progress of German troops into Poland. By the time I left for Cadgwith I was heartily sick of the news.

With a pair of lines over the side of the boat and the gentle chug-chug of the engine, I was at last able to forget that the country was living under the threat of war. And soon my whole mind was occupied with the task of landing mackerel. Big Logan stood facing me at the tiller, whistling softly through his teeth. He hardly spoke a word, except when I hauled a line in and he looked astern for the darting strip of silver that would tell him there was a mackerel on it.

We went as far as Dinas Head. As we headed back the wind began to freshen from the sou'west and little scuds of cloud appeared, flying low across the sky. By seven-thirty the light was beginning to go. 'Looks like a bad night,' I said.

'Ar, it's going to rain all right.' He rolled himself a cigarette and put the boat in towards the cliffs. 'We might have a try for pollock,' he said.

The sea was getting up and away on the starboard bow I could see the waves swirling white round a submerged rock. 'You want to know this coast pretty well,' I said.

'You're right there. It's a wicked bit of coast this—submerged rocks everywhere. And they're not rounded like they are over to Land's End, but all jagged. See the Gav Rocks over to Kennack here?' He pointed across the bows to the jagged reef, now half-submerged, that curved out across Kennack Sands. 'A Dutch barge went aground there—oh, it must have been four winters back. In three days there was nothing of her left except an iron stern post that's there to this day, wedged among the rocks.'

'Have you had any wrecks recently?' I asked. 'There was the *Clan Malcolm*, I know—but since then?'

'Not just round here. There was one over to St Ives.' He lit his cigarette. 'Now the *Clan Malcolm*, she was a lovely wreck—a real Cornishman's wreck.' He shook his head over it. 'If we had a wreck like that every year we wouldn't need to worry about the winter.' He put the tiller down and edged the boat along the shore. We were very close in now and the sea was making it difficult for me to stand. 'You might get at pollock here,' he said, taking over my other line.

But, though we circled for more than ten minutes around the spot, all I got was a snide—a cross between a baby swordfish and an eel that made the bottom of the boat abominably slimy and got thoroughly tied up in the line. At length Big Logan headed the boat out to sea again. 'You ought to get a few mackerel on the way back,' he said. At that time I had caught just on forty. The sea was getting very jumpy, and every now and then I had to sit down on the thwart for fear of losing my balance. The movement of the boat did not seem to worry Logan. With feet spread slightly apart his great hulk seemed to tread the planks and almost to steady the boat.

We were level with Caerleon Cove and about half a mile out when I got my next bite. I felt one sharp tug and then the line went quiet. I pulled it in. It was a mackerel all right. They always seemed to lie quiet after they had been hooked. I left Logan to deal with it and went over to the other line. As soon as I felt it I knew it was shoal mackerel for there was one on this line too. I began to pull it in. Suddenly there was a flash of broken water in the trough of a wave. I caught sight of it out of the corner of my eye. Something solid went streaking through the water beside the boat. The sea swirled and eddied, and before I had time to see what it was the line went tight in my hand and I was whipped overboard.

Instead of bobbing to the surface immediately, I seemed to be sucked down into the sea. I was seized with a sudden panic. My breath escaped in a rush of bubbles and with my lungs suddenly emptied, I found myself as near to drowning as I have ever been. I fought my way upwards with a horrible feeling of constriction across the chest. And when I thought I could not restrain my lungs from functioning normally any longer, I came to the surface and trod water, gasping for breath.

Almost immediately Big Logan hailed me from the boat, which had now circled and was making towards me. A moment later he had hauled me on board and I lay panting on the bottom of the boat. A fish flapped unhappily on the boards beside my head. I rolled over and found myself face to face with the mackerel that I had left Big Logan to deal with. Its plight was so similar to what mine had been an instant ago that I scooped it up in my hand and threw it back into the sea. Then I sat up and looked at Big Logan. 'What was it?' I asked.

He shook his head and tugged at his beard. 'I'd just got the mackerel off your line,' he said, 'and had dropped the weight back into the water, when suddenly the whole boat was rocking like hell and you were overboard. I looked up just in time to see your feet disappearing over the side. The line was tight in your hand, I could see that. Something pretty big must have got hold of it. It not only jerked you overboard so violently that your feet did not even touch the gun'l, but it snapped the line as clean as though it had been cut with a knife.'

The boat was now headed back towards Cadgwith, and I scrambled to my feet.

'How are you feeling?' he asked.

'Unpleasantly wet, but otherwise all right.' But I was a bit shaken and had to sit on the thwart. 'Does this sort of thing often happen?' I asked him. I glanced up and surprised a rather puzzled look on his face.

'Never known it to happen afore, sir,' he replied.

'What was it?' I persisted. 'An outsize in pollock, a tunny fish, a shark—or what?'

'Well, it might have been a tunny or a shark,' he said, a trifle doubtfully I thought. 'You had a mackerel on that line, didn't you?'

I nodded. 'And I saw something break the surface of the water just beside the boat,' I said. 'It was in the trough of a wave and moving fast in the direction of the mackerel. Would it have been the fin of a shark, do you think? Do you get sharks round this coast?'

'Sometimes. You get 'em on most coasts.' He shook his head. 'It must have been a pretty big one,' he murmured. 'You should have seen the state of the sea after you'd taken your header. It was as though a whale had submerged.'

He rolled a cigarette for me and we fell silent, smoking thoughtfully. I was beginning to feel pretty cold by the time we reached Cadgwith. As soon as we had landed he took me straight up to the pub, where I was introduced to the landlord, given a pair of old trousers and a jersey, and my wet clothes hung up to dry. I ordered a hot rum and lemon. Big Logan and the landlord joined me with whiskies and then fell to an interminable discussion of the whole business. I had already decided it was a shark and I was not interested. Sitting in front of the warm kitchen range I soon began to feel sleepy.

Big Logan had to shake me awake in order to tell me that he would take me back to Church Cove by boat. I could hear the wind howling in the chimney and I shook my head. 'I'll walk,' I said.

'Your clothes aren't dry yet and you're tired,' he said. 'Much better let me run you back. There's still a little light left and the sea isn't too bad yet.'

But I shook my head. 'Honestly, I'd like the walk,' I told him. 'It'll warm me up. That is, if you don't mind my hanging on to these clothes until tomorrow?' I asked the landlord.

'That's all right,' he said. 'You're welcome. And if you'll come over tomorrow we'll have your own clothes dry for you by then.'

I thanked him and got to my feet. I tried to pay Big Logan for the fishing trip, but he said he didn't accept money for nearly drowning people. And when I tried to insist, he thrust the pound note back into the pocket of my jacket, which I had put on, wet though it was, because it contained my wallet and my keys. He even offered to accompany me along the cliffs, but by this time I was feeling sufficiently wide awake and buoyed up by the drink to insist that I should enjoy the walk.

As he came out of the pub with me, he called to two fellows in the bar to come and help him in with his boat. The evening light was still sufficient for me to be able to see it bobbing about at its moorings. The wind was rising still and already the waves were beginning to sound noisily on the shingle beach as they tumbled into the inlet. I climbed the roadway to the cliffs and met the full force of the growing gale. I was more than ever glad then that I had not accepted Logan's offer to run me back to Church Cove.

The heat of exertion made the jersey and the rough serge trousers most uncomfortable. I had nothing on underneath them and my skin was sensitive to the rough material. Moreover, my shoes, which were still wet, squelched at every step. I found the farmyard, and climbing the stone stile, reached the path that skirted the Devil's Frying Pan. The flashing of the Lizard light was plainly visible along the coast. There was still a slight glow in the sky ahead, but despite this I found it very difficult to see the path and every now and then I was reduced literally to feeling my way along for fear I should strike out towards the edge of the cliffs.

I passed the big white house on the headland and in a little while came to a part-wooden bungalow that did service as a café. Half of a window still showed light through orange curtains, but the other half was already blacked out with brown paper. I suddenly remembered that for more than three hours I had forgotten all about the crisis. The rum seemed to recede all at once from my brain and leave me wretchedly depressed. I climbed another stone stile and followed the path inland as it circled a long indent. I followed it automatically, for my mind was entirely wrapped in a mental picture of the Western Front. And I suddenly felt that, having come so near to death that night, a merciful God should have finished the job rather than spare me to rot in a stinking trench.

I was possessed of the cowardice that is the heritage of an imaginative mind. It is anticipation and not the pain itself that breeds fear. I singled myself out for a horrible death as I trod that cliff path. In fact, from the way in which I regarded my death as inevitable one would have thought that it was for that sole purpose that Hitler had regimented Germany for six years. And when I almost stumbled into a man standing, a vague blur, on the path in front of me, I recoiled involuntarily with a little cry.

'I am sorry. I am afraid I frightened you,' he said.

'Oh, no,' I said. 'You startled me a bit, that's all. I was thinking about something else.'

'I was hoping you could direct me to a cottage called Carillon that lies back from the cliffs somewhere near here.'

'Carillon?' I murmured. Suddenly I remembered where I had seen the name. 'Is it above Church Cove?' I asked.

'That is right,' he said. His speech was so precise and impersonal that I felt he must be a B.B.C. announcer on holiday.

'If you care to come with me,' I said, 'I think I can find it for you. It lies just back from this path about half a mile further on.'

He thanked me and fell into place behind me. As I went past him I found that the rather stiff-looking waterproof he wore was soaked practically to the waist.

'You're wet,' I said.

There was a moment's pause, and then he said, 'Yes, I have been out in a boat and had some trouble getting ashore. The sea is getting quite rough.'

'Funny!' I said. 'I've just got wet through too.' And I told him about my little adventure.

Somehow I got the impression that he was rather impressed by what had happened. 'And what do you think it was?' he asked, when I had finished.

I told him I thought it must have been a shark. He had drawn level with me as the path widened, and I saw him nod. 'They are to be seen about these western coasts. It went for the mackerel.' He then referred to the crisis and asked me whether there were any fresh developments. Then he asked if I had seen anything of the fleet. I told him it had passed down the Channel a week ago and that not a single naval vessel had been seen off the coast since then, except for five destroyers and one submarine of unknown nationality.

He sighed. 'I am afraid it will be war,' he said.

I nodded. 'Oh, well,' I said, 'it's no more than one expected. But it's a bit of a shock when it comes.' I sensed that he too was depressed. 'Will you be called up?' I asked.

'I expect so.'

'What branch?'

'Navy.'

'It's better than most,' I consoled him. 'Better than the trenches.'

'Maybe,' he said, but he did not sound very enthusiastic.

For a time we walked in silence. Then to take our minds off morbid thoughts I began to talk of the coast, the submerged rocks and the wrecks. 'The fisherman I was out with today told me of a Dutch barge that was completely broken up on the Gav Rocks at Kennack in three days,' I said.

'Yes, I have been here before,' he said. 'It is a bad coast.'

I nodded. 'It is,' I agreed. 'And they say that quite a lot of the submerged rocks aren't even charted and are only known by the local fisherman.'

'I know,' was his reply. 'There is a great reef out off Cadgwith that is not properly charted. It is the worst bit of coast I think I have ever seen.'

'Of course, these fishermen know it all,' I said. 'They know just where to find a sand bottom among the rocks. I suppose the knowledge of the rock formations on the bed of the sea is handed down from father to son and grows with the knowledge gained by each new generation.' We had reached the top of a headland and a path branched off to the right, skirting a field. 'You go up there,' I said. 'The cottage is on the right.'

He thanked me and we parted, his slim erect figure merging into the gloom. I went on down into Church Cove.

2

Suspicion

'Will listeners please stand by for an important announcement which will be made at nine-fifteen.' It was early Sunday morning and even the announcer's voice sounded strained and unfamiliar. I sat in the Kerris's kitchen, smoking cigarettes and waiting. So we heard of the final two-hour ultimatum delivered by Sir Neville Henderson. Later came the news that the Prime Minister would broadcast at eleven-fifteen. Rather than hang about waiting for what I knew to be inevitable, I got the car out and drove over to Cadgwith with the clothes the landlord had lent me.

When I returned to the car, with my own clothes dried and neatly done up in brown paper, I met Big Logan coming up from the beach. 'You don't mean to say you've been out with the boats this morning?' I said. There was quite a sea running, though the wind had dropped and it was a fine morning.

He laughed. 'War or no war we've still got to earn our living,' he said. 'I hope you're none the worse for your bathe last night?'

'Not a bit,' I replied, as I threw the bundle of clothes into the back of the car. 'Funny thing was,' I added, shutting the door, 'I met a fellow on my way back to Church Cove who had also got pretty wet landing from a boat.'

'Landing from a boat?' He looked puzzled. 'Where did he land?' he asked.

I shrugged my shoulders. 'I don't know. Somewhere round here, I suppose. I met him on the path just past that little café on the cliff.'

'No boat came in here. We were the last in.'

'Well, he probably landed somewhere along the coast,' I suggested.

'Why should he do that? Nobody would think of landing anywhere between here and Church Cove with the sea as jumpy as it was last night—unless of course he had to. How wet was he?'

'I should say he had been up to his waist in water. Anyway, what does it matter?' I demanded. I was a trifle annoyed at his persistence.

He hesitated. His feet were placed slightly apart and his hands rested on the leather belt around his waist. At length he said, 'Well, I've been thinking. That business last night—how do we know it was a fish?'

'What else could it have been?' I asked impatiently.

He looked at me, and once again I was impressed by the shrewdness of his small eyes. 'It might have been a submarine,' he said.

I stared at him. 'A submarine?' Then I suddenly laughed. 'But why should a submarine jump half out of the water and pounce upon a poor inoffensive mackerel? Submarines don't have to feed. Anyway, it would be dangerous to come so close in without surfacing.'

'Did it jump half out of the water?' he asked, and I saw that he was perfectly serious. 'Are you certain it was after the mackerel?'

'Perhaps jumping half out of the water is an exaggeration,' I admitted, 'but at least I saw a fin or something streak through the water in the trough of a wave.'

'Or something,' he said. 'Mightn't it have been a periscope?'

I thought about this for a moment. 'I suppose it might,' I agreed. 'But why should it take my line?'

'The line might have got caught up in the submarine.'

'But it's absurd,' I said.

'You didn't see the water after you'd taken that header. It boiled as though a bloody whale had gone down. The disturbance was too much for a shark. Anyway, that's what I think.'

'But, whatever would it be doing so close in?' I asked.

'That's what's been puzzling me,' he said. 'But you mentioning that fellow you met having got so wet has given me an idea. They might have wanted to land someone.'

I thought this over for a moment. It was not altogether fantastic. And yet it seemed incredible. Looking back, I think that what seemed so incredible to me was not the presence of the submarine, but the fact that I had become involved in its presence. I am not accustomed to being caught up in violent adventures. My job is to comment on drama, not take part in it, and I felt somehow a little sceptical of my being knocked overboard by a submarine.

'Did the fellow you met say anything to you?' Big Logan asked.

'Yes, he asked me the way to a cottage called Carillon, which stands back from the cliffs above Church Cove.' It was then that I remembered his perfect English, and suddenly it seemed to me that it was almost too perfect. Word for word, as far as I could remember it, I repeated my conversation with the man.

The conversation seemed harmless enough. But Big Logan was plainly excited. 'How did he know there was a hidden reef off Cadgwith?' he demanded.

'He'd been down here before,' I pointed out. 'It may have been you yourself who told him. He probably went out fishing.'

'Then can you tell me how he knew it wasn't properly charted?'

I couldn't, but at the same time I was by no means convinced that this made the man a spy. Nevertheless, I was glad Big Logan had not realized that in conversation with this stranger I had given him important information concerning the movement of the fleet. Anyway, I consoled myself, if he were a spy he would have the information soon enough.

'I suggest we go along and have a word with Joe,' Logan said. 'He knows everybody around these parts. He'll be able to tell us about the people who own this cottage.'

I followed him back into the pub. We found the landlord in the bar. He had been going over his stock and he had the radio on. He put his fingers to his lips as we went in. Two of his visitors were sitting listening.

'This morning the British Ambassador in Berlin handed the German Government a final note stating that unless we heard from them by eleven o'clock that they are prepared at once to withdraw their troops from Poland a state of war would exist between us. I have to tell you that no such undertaking has been received and that consequently this country is at war with Germany.'

The voice was Chamberlain's. The fact of war came as no great shock to me. It had been a certainty for the past twenty-four hours. Yet my stomach turned over within me at the actuality of it.

The Premier's speech was followed by announcements, commencing with details of the sounding of air raid sirens. The two visitors got up and left the bar, one saying that he was going to telephone his brother. When they had gone, Big Logan turned to the landlord. 'Do you know who lives at Carillon now, Joe? It must be over two years since Mrs Bloy died.'

'Nearer three,' replied the landlord. 'Old man of the name of Cutner has owned it ever since. Retired bank manager, I think. What do you want to know for?'

Big Logan hesitated, and then said, 'Oh, nothing—this gentleman wanted to know, that's all.' He caught me looking at him in some surprise and glanced hurriedly away. 'Know whether he has many visitors?'

'How should I know?' The landlord was looking at him curiously.

'No, of course you wouldn't. I was only——' He stopped

short. The three of us glanced round the room uneasily, aware of a sudden change. I think we all realized what it was at the same moment, for we turned and stared at the radio set at the far end of the bar. The current was still on and we could hear it crackling, but the air had gone dead. At the same moment the visitor who had gone out to phone his brother came in with an anxious look on his face to say that the local exchange could get no answer from London.

He and I were the only ones who leaped immediately to the obvious conclusion. I thought of Bloomsbury with its old houses. They would be absolute death traps. And the trees and the Georgian houses in Mecklenburg Square—should I see those again as I had known them? 'If it is a raid,' I said, 'it's quick work.'

'Perhaps it's only a test,' he said.

'Or just a coincidence,' I murmured. 'The B.B.C. is working under emergency conditions and London is probably inundated with calls.'

'Yes, that's probably it.' His voice did not carry much conviction. Later, of course, we heard that an air raid warning had been sounded, but the possibility of both radio and telephone systems having broken down at the same time enabled us to continue our conversation while the visitor went back to the phone to try again.

Big Logan steered off the subject of the owner of Carillon without any explanation as to why he had been interested in the man. We had a drink on the house and, after discussing the war for a while, we left the pub.

Outside, Big Logan said, 'We'd best go up and have a talk with Ted Morgan.' Morgan was one of the coastguards and it was plain that my companion was not feeling too sure of himself. He had not told the landlord about his suspicions, and had thus prevented the story from circulating throughout the village. Clearly he now wanted confirmation of the conclusion he had arrived at. The coastguard was the sort of father of all wisdom in the village.

But when I was introduced to him in the Board of Trade hut on the cliffs, I doubted whether he was as shrewd as Big Logan. In their relations with the Government, however, the fishermen of the village always turned to Morgan, since he understood the regulations and knew all about the forms they had to fill in. The habit had stuck.

Big Logan told him the whole story. With his feet thrust slightly apart and his thumbs in his leather waistbelt, he seemed to fill the whole hut, his beard wagging up and down as he spoke. By comparison, the little Welshman, seated at the desk before the telescope, seemed very small indeed. When Logan had finished I sensed that Morgan was sceptical. He put his head on one side like a bird and drummed with his fingers on the desk. 'It is possible, of course,' he conceded, and he darted a glance at the big fisherman. 'It is possible. I saw what I think was a U-boat about six miles off the coast only yesterday.' He leaned forward in his chair. 'But where would he have landed?'

'What about the Devil's Frying Pan?' suggested Logan.

'Yes, indeed—but it was very choppy last night. The boat would have been stove in.'

'They have collapsible boats,' replied Logan. 'They're made of rubber.'

'Well, supposing it was possible to land a man safely from a submarine at the Frying Pan, why should the Germans want to? Surely they would have all their spies in the country by now?'

It was a very reasonable point. Logan shrugged his great shoulders. 'I'm not responsible for their actions,' he said. 'Maybe this man Cutner is a spy and one of the officers of the U-boat was sent ashore to collect important information from him.'

The coastguard considered this for a moment whilst he explored his small discoloured teeth wih a toothpick. At length he shook his head and said, 'You know, there are sharks on this coast.'

'Good God Almighty!' exclaimed Big Logan with sudden exasperation. 'Do you think I don't know a bloody shark when I see one? This wasn't a shark. The displacement of water was too great. It was either a submarine or a whale. And if you think you've ever seen a whale from this little perch of yours, you'd better put in for your discharge right now.'

This outburst apparently left the little coastguard unmoved. He continued to drum with his fingers on his desk and to pick his teeth with the toothpick. In the end he turned to me and said, 'What do you think about it, Mr Craig?'

His question put me in an awkward situation. I was not at all convinced that Logan was right. It seemed much too fantastic. On the other hand, I did not want to offend him. I said, 'I think the matter ought to be investigated.'

The coastguard then turned to Logan. 'What would you like me to do about it? Get on to the police?'

'What the hell's the good of the police?' demanded Logan. 'Either get on to the Admiralty, or phone Scotland Yard and tell them to pass the information on to M.I.5.' It was only then that I realized that he must be old enough to have been through the last war. Generally the inhabitants of English country districts call it the secret service. 'If you don't feel like doing either of these,' he continued, 'I suggest we settle the matter locally.'

'How?'

'Well, figure it out this way,' he said. 'You're probably right when you say a spy wouldn't be landed by submarine—certainly not on this part of the coast. If he is a German, then he'll have been landed to collect information. And if he's been landed to collect information, he's still got to get it back to the submarine. Our job is to see that he doesn't.'

'He may have rejoined his boat already,' I said.

'What—last night?' Big Logan shook his head. 'The sea was rising fast. By the time he'd reached the cottage and got back to the shore again it would have been absolutely impossible to get a boat in anywhere along the cliffs there. It would have been pretty bad landing at Cadgwith even. What I suggest is, we lie in wait for him on the cliffs above the Frying Pan tonight. If he doesn't come—well then, we can consider what's best to be done.'

The coastguard considered this. Then he said, 'All right, Big Logan. You and Mr Craig here wait for him on the cliffs. I'll take two of the boys and keep watch by the head there.' He nodded through the window to the opposite headland that guarded the entrance to Cadgwith from the south west. 'I suppose we can take your boat?'

Big Logan nodded. 'Surely. And take that old service revolver of yours, Ted—you may need it.'

The coastguard pulled open a drawer and, routing among a pile of government forms and other papers, produced a revolver. He turned it over reflectively in his hand as though it brought back old memories. Then he shook his head. 'It's early for spy scares. Still, it won't do any harm to take it along.'

So it was that at nine-thirty that evening Big Logan and I met on the path above the Devil's Frying Pan. By that time I had heard the news of the sinking of the *Athenia* and was suffering from that indefinable desire to express my horror in action. This, I think, is the most deadly moral effect of war. As I had walked along the path from Church Cove my mind had evolved all sorts of wild schemes by which I could bring about the destruction of the submarine. It wasn't until I had settled down to the long vigil on the cliff-top that I gave a thought for the men in the boat itself. Then all the horror of the *Thetis* disaster flooded back into my mind. Journalism and the theatre foster the growth of an imagination. And in war an imagination is a definite handicap. I could not help—despite the sinking of the *Athenia*—a sudden feeling of deep sympathy for men of the German submarine service scattered about the high seas, cooped up in their steel shells, facing a horrible and almost inevitable death.

But after all, there was no question of destroying the submarine. Somehow I felt thankful that Big Logan had not felt sure enough of himself to insist upon the Admiralty being notified. I could picture the torpedo boat waiting under the shelter of the headland and then dashing out, as the U-boat submerged, to drop depth charges that would blow her back to the surface and destroy her utterly. But there was only Big Logan's boat waiting, with no bigger armaments than the coastguard's revolver, and the two of us sitting on top of the cliffs. Anyway, there probably was no U-boat.

That belief grew as the hours slipped monotonously by. We could neither smoke nor talk. We sat on a great rock on the westward side of the Frying Pan, watching the sea until everything merged into the blackness of a tunnel. There were no stars, no moon—the night was like a pit. I had brought some chocolate. We ate that, spinning it out as long as possible, for it gave us something to do. At length I began to feel drowsy. It was then nearly two. I was cold and stiff. For a time I felt angry with Big Logan for assuming that I would accompany him on this damfool errand. The belief that he did not know a shark when he saw one had grown to a certainty by the time I fell asleep.

It seemed but a second later that I was being shaken out of my sleep. I opened my mouth to speak, but a rough hand closed over it and Big Logan's voice whispered in my ear, 'Keep quiet and watch the sea.'

I felt suddenly tense. The night was as black as ever and, as I stared out into it, I felt that I might just as well be blind. Then suddenly a light showed out there on the water. I saw its reflection for an instant in the sea. Then it was gone, and the night was as dark as ever, so that I felt it must have been my imagination.

Big Logan did not move. I sensed the rigidity of his body. His head, only a few feet away from my own, was just visible.

It was tilted slightly to one side as he listened, his eyes fixed on the spot where I supposed the water must flow into the Frying Pan.

At length he rose. And I scrambled to my feet too, though I had heard nothing. He took my arm and together we moved with great care back on to the path. There we waited, huddled against the wall of the big white house that lay back from the Frying Pan. 'The boat has arrived,' he whispered in my ear. 'It's down in the Frying Pan now. And I saw the flash of your friend's torch away along the cliff as he signalled the submarine.'

It seemed hours before we heard the sound of footsteps on the path. Actually I suppose it was only a few minutes. They drew nearer. I felt Logan tense for the spring. Then they ceased. Almost at the same time there was the flash of a torch reddened by a screening hand. And in that flash the slim waterproof-clad figure stood out quite clearly. He had left the path and had reached almost the exact spot where we had been sitting. He was descending the steep shoulder of the Frying Pan towards the archway.

For all his bulk, Logan moved swiftly. He was down the slope, a vague blur in the darkness, almost before I had crossed the path. As I scrambled down the shoulder I saw him pounce. It was so dark that it was difficult to distinguish what happened, but I think the man turned just before the attack. My one fear had been that he would have a revolver. But if he had, he got no chance to use it. Logan had the advantage of the slope and his own huge bulk. They went down together, and when I reached them Logan had his man pinioned to the ground, his hand across his mouth. 'Search him,' he said.

I ran my hands over his body and felt the outline of an automatic in the pocket of his waterproof. I was on the point of removing it when the whole scene was suddenly illuminated by a torch. I looked up and was almost blinded by its light. I have a vivid mental picture of Big Logan's bearded head in silhouette against that dazzling light. The light came steadily nearer. A tall man in uniform was standing over us. His arms rose and fell, and as it fell in front of the torch I saw that his hand grasped a big service revolver by the barrel. There was a sickening thud, and Big Logan slumped forward. The man in the waterproof thrust Logan's body away from him and scrambled to his feet. Something cold and hard was pressed against my head. I knew what it was and I thought my last hour had come. The man had not switched off his torch and I could see Big Logan's head hanging loosely over a rock and blood was trickling down from his scalp into his beard. I thought the blow had killed him.

'*Wir werden sie beide mitnehmen.*' It was the man in the waterproof speaking. I was never so thankful for a knowledge of German. Their decision to take us along was presumably due to a desire to leave no evidence of the fact that they had landed and to safeguard, as far as possible, the owner of Carillon.

The man in the waterproof turned to me. 'You must regard yourself as our prisoner,' he said in his precise English. 'You will walk two paces in front. Any attempt to escape or to attract attention and you will be shot.' He motioned me forward with his automatic, and then he and the other German each took hold of one of Logan's arms. The torch was switched off and in the sudden darkness I could hardly see where I was going. I could hear Logan's feet dragging along the ground behind me as I went down the slope to the bottom of the Frying Pan. The Germans frequently had to pause in order to adjust Logan's weight between them and the sound of their breathing became louder.

It grew darker than ever as we descended and I almost stumbled into the arms of a man waiting at the water's edge. He challenged us in German. '*Schon gut, Karl,*' answered the man in the waterproof. '*Sehen Sie, dass die Leute in's Boot kommen.*'

'*Zu Befehl, Herr Kapitaenlautnent.*'

So Logan had been right. It was the commander of the U-boat that had been landed. I began to wonder what it was that he had come ashore for. It must have been something of considerable importance for him to run that risk at the outbreak of war. We ought to have realized that one of the boat's crew might come up to meet him. Our only hope now lay in the coastguard, waiting off the headland—or had they already dealt with him? Was that what had put them on their guard?

The boat was dragged in closer. It was a collapsible affair with two oars, and by the time Logan's inert body had been placed in it, there seemed no prospect of it holding four more men. However, it did, though it sat very low in the water as a result. The commander sat facing me with his automatic ready, while the other two men took an oar each.

Silently we slid beneath the great archway that had originally formed the entrance to the cave before it had collapsed to make the Frying Pan. It was lighter as soon as we got out into the open sea and it was possible to distinguish the dim outline of the cliffs towering above us. Soon, however, even this landmark merged and was lost in the night. It seemed impossible to believe that we should find the submarine in the dark until, turning my head, I saw the merest pinprick of a light showing straight over our bows.

I looked back at the commander. He was watching me, the automatic gripped in his hand, its barrel pointed at me. Big Logan lay inert between us. There was no sign of the coastguard's boat. Then I began to think of the information that the U-boat commander had presumably obtained. What was it—movements of merchant ships, fleet dispositions, transport sailings? It might mean the loss of hundreds of lives if he were allowed to reach the submarine with it. I shifted my position. The boat rocked dangerously. 'Still!' Though the commander spoke English, his voice was not English. There was something cold about it, and I sat rigid, the automatic thrust a few inches nearer.

But it was my life and possibly Big Logan's against the lives of many others. On me lay the responsibility for action. I hesitated. Then suddenly I made up my mind. I would jump on the side of the boat. It was bound to capsize. Then anything might happen. I tensed my muscles for the spring.

And at that moment I heard the roar of a powerful engine. A searchlight suddenly stretched out a white pencil of light across the water. It swept round in a short arc and came to rest on the rubber boat, blinding us completely. The drone of the engines grew louder and then came the rattle of machine gun fire. Little spouts of water flew up all round us. One of the men at the oars slumped into the bottom of the boat, almost capsizing it.

The searchlight bore rapidly down on us. The boat's intention was obvious. It was going to ram us. Close behind us came a sudden ear-splitting explosion. A huge spout of water flew up white in the searchlight. Another flung spray right over the advancing boat. It veered away and I saw the grey lines of a British torpedo boat flash past our stern, the water swirling up from its bows. Before I had time to do anything the steel bows of a submarine nosed alongside.

The commander jumped out on to the deck, which was half awash. In an instant I found myself hauled out of the boat and bundled towards the conning tower. I passed the for'ard gun just as it fired again and my ears went completely deaf. As I was thrust down the conning tower hatch I saw the torpedo boat swing in a great arc. Its searchlight suddenly went out and everything was black. The commander dropped down beside me, shouting a string of orders so fast that I could not understand them. Immediately the submarine's engines came to life and she began to swing sharply to port. I knew then that the commander was afraid of being torpedoed and I felt a sudden emptiness inside me.

Logan's great body, still unconscious, was thrust down the hatch almost on top of me. We were pushed out of the way and the crew scrambled down, two carrying the man who had been hit. The hatch closed with a bang. The sound of the engines immediately seemed like a great throbbing pulse. It was very warm and there was a strong smell of oil. We were bundled into two bunks out of the way. Every man was at his action station.

The boat seemed to shudder as she gathered way. A bell sounded, and a few seconds later the floor took a decided tilt. We were diving. It was a crash dive and the roar of the electric motors took the place of the diesels. We were no sooner on an even keel than I sensed rather than actually felt the boat turning. I had read enough about submarine experiences in the Great War to know what the commander was trying to avoid. The muscles of my face contracted in anticipation and my hands were clenched so tight that the nails bit into the palms.

A second later it came—a terrific crash. The U-boat bucked as though it had hit a rock and there was the sound of breaking crockery. The lights went out and, with the fuses blown, the motors stopped. There was a sudden deathly stillness. And in that stillness it was just possible to hear the drone of the torpedo boat's propellers on the surface of the sea above us. The emergency lighting came on. The shock of the depth charge had rolled Logan out of his bunk into the gangway. He picked himself up, fully conscious now. Then he saw me and said, 'My head feels bloody. There are sort of explosions going on inside it. It feels as though it will burst.'

I was about to enlighten him when a second depth charge exploded. It was not so near as the other, but even so the U-boat rocked violently for the trim was bad. The bows seemed to dip and then there was an ominous jar for'ard. Logan took one look round the place and understood. He was like a drunkard that has suddenly been sobered up by danger. His eyes cleared and he was instantly alert.

The commander shouted some order. Two seamen dashed down the gangway, pushing Logan to one side. They were followed by the man who had knocked Logan out. He was the first-lieutenant. For a moment everything seemed pandemonium. Orders were shouted and men rushed aft. Then there was quiet. Water was flooding in from the control room. The crew were on the hand gear for everything to save noise. The only sound was a gramophone playing '*Deutschland, Deutschland über Alles.*' For the second time that night I found myself thinking of the *Thetis* disaster, but there was little comfort in Professor Haldane's assurance at the enquiry that the men would not have suffered greatly.

The regulating tank had been flooded and the submarine was now on an even keel. I found I had scrambled out of my bunk. The Number One came back along the gangway shouting, '*Die Kammer achtern ist unter Wasser, nud Wasser dringt in den Maschinenraum.*'

'Do you understand what he said?' asked Logan.

'He said the stern compartment is flooded and water is coming into the engine room,' I told him.

Then there was a report of water coming in for'ard. But by this time the leak in the control room had been stopped. Two more depth charges boomed in the distance. The commander came out of the control room and was met by the engineer officer. He reported engine room leak stopped, but port motor damaged. One of the watchkeepers who was down with 'flu walked dazedly past along the gangway in his pyjamas. 'What's happened?' he asked.

'Plenty—your temperature is a hundred and two,' came the answer. 'Report to your bunk.' Then to the engineer officer, the commander said, 'What about the starboard motor?'

'Propeller shaft fractured.'

'Well, see if you can get the port motor working.'

The commander then had a long talk with his second. Part of it I could not catch. But the gist of the second's remarks gave me some idea of what had happened following the first depth charge. The explosion had apparently blown open the engine-room hatch allowing a huge volume of water to enter. Then the pressure of water from outside had sealed the hatch completely. Moreover, it appeared that the boat was now far too heavy and bobbing about between fifty and sixty feet. 'We'll have to empty the bilges,' the commander decided suddenly, 'even if the oil does give our position away.'

The second gave the order, and soon even a layman like myself could realize that the boat was lighter and more manageable. Then the second and the commander bent over a chart. I could just see them from where I was seated on my bunk. I think the commander must have sensed me watching him, for he looked up and his gaze swung from me to Logan. Then he strode down the gangway. He was still dressed in civilian clothes and wearing his stiff military-looking waterproof though the interior of the submarine was getting extremely hot. He stopped opposite Logan. 'You are a fisherman, are you not?' he asked.

Logan looked up and nodded.

'Well, I do not expect you want to die any more than we do,' the commander said. 'I should be glad if you would help us. We are lying at about fifty feet. The motors are out of action and that torpedo boat of yours is somewhere up above waiting for us. We dare not surface. But we do not know the drift so close to the shore. If we stay down we may pile ourselves up on the rocks. I calculate that at the moment we are less than a quarter of a mile off the entrance to Cadgwith.'

Big Logan stroked his beard and looked across at me. I felt a sudden excitement. It was almost exultation. I think he sensed it, for he turned to the commander, grinning all over his face. 'You've given me a crack on the head and dragged me on board this blasted tin fish of yours,' he said, 'and now you want me to get you out of the mess you've got yourself into.'

'Pardon me, but it was you who got us into this mess—or

rather your friend here. We did not arrange for a British torpedo boat to be waiting for us.'

'Torpedo boat, was it?' Big Logan suddenly clicked his fingers. 'Well, I'm damned,' he said. 'So Ted Morgan took my word for it after all. And he wanted me to believe it was a shark.' He poked a large forefinger into the U-boat commander's ribs. 'It wasn't this gentleman—' he indicated me—'that gave you away. It was your bloody submarine coming up right under my boat when he and I were out after mackerel last night. A shark! Well, I'm damned!' And suddenly he began to laugh. He laughed until the tears ran down his cheeks. The crew gathered round, staring at him. I think they thought he had gone off his head with fright.

At length, weak with laughter, he said, 'And here you are, like a lot of stuck pigs, just because you interfered with this gentleman's fishing.' I thought he was going off into another paroxysm of laugher. But suddenly he sobered up. 'Know what I'll do?' he said. 'I'll make a bargain with you—the papers you got from your friend at Carillon for information about the currents.'

I thought the commander would strike him. He was a young man and Logan had made him furious. He was a nice looking lad, very slim and erect, but he had the Prussian features and the Prussian lack of any sense of humour. The joke was on him and he could not see it. 'You are a prisoner,' he said. His voice was cold and precise. 'You will do as you are told.'

'I'll see you on the Gav Rocks first,' was Big Logan's reply. And he began to bellow with laughter again.

The commander's hand came up instantly and smacked Logan first on one cheek and then on the other. Logan's answer was instantaneous. He laid the commander out with one blow of his huge fist.

The second immediately drew his revolver. I read Logan's death sentence in his eyes and at the same time one of the crew seized me from behind. But as the second raised the gun it was struck out of his hand by another officer who had appeared behind him. It was the navigating officer. 'Don't be a fool,' he said in German. 'He's our only chance of getting out of this alive.'

Then he turned to Logan and said in broken English, 'Eet ees the lifes of you and dese other gentleman who ees at stake, as well as our own. Will you not help us? The torpedo boat, she will wait all night for us. Eef we could drift half a mile down the coast without wrecking ourselfs we could surface. Then we should be all right.'

Logan's reply was, 'I've told this officer'—he indicated the inert figure of the commander—'what my terms for helping you are. I've lived by the sea all my life and I'm not afraid to die by it, even if it is in a glorified sardine tin.'

'And that goes for me too,' I said. It was a heroic little gesture for my stomach felt queasy at the thought of death by suffocation. I suppose most people with any imagination possess a mild form of claustrophobia, but I must say that Logan's phrase about a glorified sardine tin struck home.

The navigating officer, whom I guessed to be a far more human individual and consequently a much better reader of character, immediately took Logan at his word and set about reviving the commander. This took several minutes, for Logan's whole weight had been behind the punch.

The man eventually staggered to his feet, but he was so dazed by the blow that it was several minutes before the navigating officer could make him understand the position. When he did he blazed up in a fury. 'You have the audacity to try to make terms with me,' he cried, turning on Logan. But he kept his distance this time. 'You come aboard this ship as a prisoner, you behave like a lunatic, strike the commander and then expect to barter information which you possess on fantastic terms.' He gave an order to the crew. Three of them closed in on Logan. Logan remained calm and impassive, but his little grey eyes roamed the narrow gangway, gauging distances and possibilities. It looked like a real scrap.

The navigating officer, however, continued to talk in low tones with the commander. The two men were of completely contrasting types. The navigating officer was small in height and rather stocky, with a round ruddy face that spoke of years at sea. The commander, on the other hand, was a typical Nazi— excitable, overbearing and cold-blooded. However, the navigating officer apparently got his way, for the commander turned to Logan and said, 'If you help us, we will land you and your companion on shore as soon as it is safe to do so.'

I pictured the surface of the sea, the towering cliffs, Cadgwith and the green fields beyond. What a relief it would be to get out of this little nightmare world of machinery that reeked of oil and was so hot and stuffy. A word or two from Logan and we were safe. He glanced at me. Something stubborn and perverse seemed to rise up within me. I shook my head. He nodded and smiled. 'We want the papers,' he said.

The commander swung round on him. 'Well, you won't get them—understand that.'

'Then neither will your superiors,' Logan answered quietly.

When the fury of a man's emotions gets the better of him and he is at the same time baffled, it is not a pretty sight. I wondered how long his nerves would hold out against the incessant tension of service in U-boats. The strain had been too great for a number of submarine commanders in the last war.

At last he mastered himself sufficiently to say, 'Very well, we'll stay down for half an hour.'

'And send yourself and your crew to certain death?' asked Logan. He looked at me. 'That serves our purpose just as well, eh?'

I had to agree with him, though I felt like being sick.

The commander tried to bluster for a moment. 'You are bluffing,' he shouted angrily.

Logan shrugged his shoulders. 'You'd best call my bluff, if you think so.'

The man's uneasiness, however, got the better of him. He stood watching Logan for some seconds and then he said, 'All right. I'll get you the papers.' He turned and strode down the gangway to the officers' quarters.

I looked at Logan, wondering what good it would do to get hold of the papers since the man might very well have a copy or have memorized them. 'Why don't you keep silent and let them run on the rocks?' I asked in a whisper.

'Because,' he replied, 'the drift of the current here is seaward. They're as safe as houses, if they only knew it. If we can't get an undertaking from them to wireless the information through to Fort Blockhouse, then we'll have to try and scare them into surfacing and hope that the torpedo boat will still be around.'

The prospect seemed pretty grim.

It was some time before the commander returned. He held in his hand a single sheet of paper. This he handed to the navigating officer, who passed it on to Logan. 'Now step up here and explain the drift on the chart,' the commander said.

Logan glanced at the sheet of paper and then held it out so that I could also read it. I cannot remember all the details of it. But it gave the position, longitude and latitude, of a rendezvous for three separate squadrons of British ships—one from Gibraltar, one from the Atlantic and one from Portsmouth. Logan explained to me that the rendezvous was about thirty miles south of the Shambles Light—that is off Portland. Those coming from Gibraltar and the Atlantic were largely capital ships. Those coming from Portsmouth were mainly destroyers and minesweepers.

Logan placed his big forefinger on the list of those coming from the Atlantic. 'They're short of destroyers,' he said. 'Until they meet up with the Portsmouth boats those four battleships will be insufficiently screened. What a chance for the U-boats!'

There were certainly not nearly so many destroyers and

torpedo boats with this squadron as with that coming up from Gibraltar. My eyes travelled on down the paper. The rendezvous was for Monday, September 18 at 13.30 hours. The object of the gathering was to sweep up the Channel, pass through the Downs and carry out a raid on the Kiel Canal. Blockships were to be waiting in the Downs and these were to be sunk in the canal if it proved possible to silence the shore batteries. Raids by Bomber Command of the R.A.F. were to accompany the attack and three fighter squadrons would co-operate in preventing enemy aircraft from harassing the raiding fleet.

As I grasped the magnitude and daring of the plan, I could not help being amazed at the ability of the German secret service to obtain information of such a vitally secret nature. 'Have they got a chance of sinking those four battleships?' I asked.

'Quite a good chance, I should say,' Logan replied. 'And if there are enough U-boats in this vicinity they might have a shot at the main gathering.'

Our conversation was interrupted by the commander. 'Stop that whispering,' he ordered, 'and let us have the information we require.'

Logan strode down the gangway towards the control room. 'Certainly,' he said, 'if you'll transmit a message to Fort Blockhouse, Portsmouth.'

The commander's eyes narrowed. 'You have the information I obtained. Keep your side of the bargain.'

'You know my purpose in requiring this information before directing you to safety,' Logan answered. 'My intention was to prevent its use by the enemies of my country. If you have a copy of this or if you have memorized——'

'I have neither copied it nor memorized it,' the other cut in.

'In that case there is no objection to your sending my message to the Admiralty.'

The commander moved forward. There was something stealthy, almost cat-like in the way he moved. 'I will not be called a liar in my own ship—certainly not by a *verflucht* Britisher. You have the insolence to demand that this ship's radio be used to transmit messages to the British Naval authorities. I'll see you in hell first.'

'Then, you won't have long to wait,' was Logan's reply.

The navigating officer, who had been following the conversation intently, said, 'Eet will be your lifes as well as ours.'

'If these ships meet as arranged,' Logan replied, tapping the paper in his hand, 'it may mean the loss of hundreds of lives. It's our lives against theirs. We prefer that it should be two and not several hundred British lives that are lost. So it's Davy Jones for you if you don't give me a solemn pledge to radio my warning to the authorities as soon as I have got you out of this mess and you have a chance to dry off your aerials.'

'As you wish,' said the commander. There was something of a sneer in his voice. I think he thought we might crack up under the strain, for after he had barked out an order in German he stood watching us. The hiss of the compressed air entering the tanks of the submarine, forcing the water out, was incredibly loud. It seemed to fill my ears.

'Now do you still withhold the information we need? If you do, I am going to surface and take a chance with this torpedo boat of yours.' And when neither of us answered, the commander shrugged his shoulders. 'Gun crews stand by!' he ordered in German. Then he disappeared up into the conning tower.

The next few minutes were some of the most unpleasant I have ever experienced. It was not difficult to sense the tension in the submarine. The atmosphere was by now getting very heavy and I was sweating like a pig with the heat of the place. The hiss of the compressed air gradually lessened. The second officer adjusted the trim. The submarine had risen on an even keel and was now, I presumed, lying at periscope depth while the commander watched the torpedo boat and chose his time.

I wondered whether the port diesel had been affected or not. If it had, then we were for it.

The commander's voice suddenly called out, 'Blow all tanks! Surface!' The compressed air hissed in the tanks and the boat shot up so quickly that I could hear the sea water flooding back from the deck. '*Geschuetzmannschaften auf Bereitschaft!*' The gun crews swarmed like monkeys into the conning tower. The hatch slammed back and feet sounded over our heads. Then the one diesel engine began to throb and the ship shuddered as the bows bit into the waves.

The gun crews would be at their stations now. I could hear the swirl of the water overhead and I presumed we were travelling with decks awash in order to keep the boat steady. The U-boat's surface speed of 18 knots was reduced, Big Logan reckoned, to about 9 or 10 as a result of the damage to the starboard propeller shaft. The speed of the torpedo boat, on the other hand, was well over 40 knots. We had not long to wait. A bell sounded in the engine room. The pulsing of the single engine grew more and more frenzied. The whole ship seemed to be shaking and rattling. The din was incredible. Then suddenly there was a sharp detonation and we were almost thrown off our feet. For a moment I thought we had been hit by a torpedo. But I had barely recovered my balance when the explosion was repeated and I realized that it was the after gun being fired. So the torpedo boat had spotted us and we were in action!

To analyse my hopes during the minutes that followed is quite impossible. I was torn between the desire for self-preservation and what I sensed to be my duty. The two were completely irreconcilable. I have, however, a vivid recollection of growing horror at the idea of being imprisoned and suffocated in that infernal U-boat, and towards the end of the action I must admit that that was my dominating thought. I must have been in a pitiable state of funk by the end for I remember nothing about it except that I babbled incoherent nonsense whilst Logan shook me till my teeth rattled in order to prevent me from going completely off my head.

It was a most unpleasant experience, and as an exhibition it must have been disgusting. Strangely enough, it did not make it impossible for me afterwards to go in a submarine again. In fact, those twenty minutes seemed to sweat all terror of death by suffocation out of me. Logan, on the other hand, preserved that same calm throughout the engagement, though he informed me afterwards that he had never actually been in a submarine before. All his experience of submarine warfare in the last war had been gained on minesweepers and coastal patrols, and later on 'Q' ships.

I do not remember much about that engagement. All that remains vivid in my mind is the throb of the engines, which seemed to pulse right through me, the draught from the open conning tower hatch, the incessant gunfire and my own terror. I remember that a few minutes from the outset the after gun crew ceased firing. But they remained at their stations and some ten minutes later the for'ard gun opened fire and at the same time the commander ordered an eight point turn to starboard—eight points represent a right-angle. I think it was this order that really finished me, for I was pretty certain that it meant a torpedo had been launched at us.

Later, I learned from listening to the conversation of the officers and men that we had surfaced about half a mile out off Caerleon Cove, which lies just east of Cadgwith. The torpedo boat was still off Cadgwith, but within a few seconds her searchlight had picked up the U-boat. The torpedo boat had immediately extinguished her searchlight. The commander, explaining the action to the navigating officer later, said that the drone of the torpedo boat's engines was plainly audible from the conning tower even above the sound of the U-boat's own engine. The order had been given for the U-boat's searchlight to be switched on and as soon as it had picked out the attacking craft the after gun crew had opened fire.

The U-boat was then travelling almost due east with the torpedo boat dead astern. Shortly afterwards the gun crew scored what looked like a direct hit and the torpedo boat swerved off its course and was lost to sight. The U-boat then made a turn of sixteen points and doubled back in the hope of shaking off the torpedo boat if it were still in action.

What actually happened I have pieced together from a talk I had some months later with the coastguard who was on board the torpedo boat. After getting out of range of the U-boat's searchlight, the boat had hove-to and listened for the sound of the submarine's engine. As they had expected, the U-boat's searchlight was extinguished and it began to double back. By this time the clouds had thinned and a rather pale young moon had appeared. As the U-boat approached they got under way with their engines just ticking over and moved up between the shore and the U-boat, endeavouring to merge their craft into the background of the cliffs. This proved so successful that they had actually manoeuvred into position and fired their torpedo before they were sighted. In actual fact, it was the torpedo, and not the torpedo boat, that the U-boat commander first sighted, for the wake of the torpedo showed like a streak of silver in the moonlight. It was then that the order for an eight point turn was made. At the same time our own searchlight picked out the torpedo boat and the for'ard gun opened fire. As the submarine swung on to her new course the after gun crew took up the fire. The torpedo apparently almost scraped the U-boat's side.

The gun crew had the range almost immediately this time and their third shot hit the sea just behind the torpedo boat, seriously damaging the engines and injuring one man. At the same time our port look-out reported a ship on the port bow. All he had seen was the white bow wave. But through his glasses the commander picked out the shape of a destroyer coming at full tilt to the scene of action.

Down in the bowels of the U-boat we heard orders being

shouted and then the clatter of sea boots on the deck plates above our heads. The men came tumbling down through the conning tower, the hatch cover slammed to and in a few seconds I was experiencing my second crash dive of the evening.

This time, however, we were far enough out for the commander to have complete confidence in the charts. There was apparently a sand bottom and the dive was straightened out, the boat trimmed and we settled slowly on to the bed of the sea. For nearly an hour we could hear the ugly boom of depth charges in the distance. None came very near us, however, and we settled down to a long vigil.

I think it was this long vigil that really cured me of my terror. Time dulls the senses and in the end I settled down to a game of cards. That we were allowed, as prisoners, to indulge in a game of cards by a commander who obviously could not regard us in too friendly a light may seem surprising. I think my own exhibition of terror was the cause. Fear is catching, and fear in a submarine at a time of emergency is to be avoided at all costs.

That game of poker must constitute something of a record. It started at three o'clock in the morning and it went on, subject to various interruptions, until nearly midnight the following night. We sat or reclined on the bunks and for a table we had a packing case from the store chamber. The light, which was directly above us, threw the interior of the bunks into complete darkness, so that it was impossible to see anyone's features, and even when they leaned forward to put their cards down it only shone on the tops of their heads. The contrast between Logan's head and those of the Germans who played with us remains very vivid in my mind. His hair stood up like a great mop, which together with his beard, gave him a very wild look. The Germans, on the other hand, had close-cropped heads and even those whose overalls were blackened with oil still managed to look quite smart.

The navigation officer played with us most of the time, acting as interpreter. At Logan's suggestion I pretended that I did not understand a word of German, a pretence which was to stand us in good stead later. Different members of the crew joined us at various times. They gave us the benefit of the tourist rate of exchange for our money. Nobody seemed to feel like sleep until well into the next day.

I began to feel drowsy, however, quite soon after breakfast, which was an excellent meal of pressed ham and hard boiled eggs. For a time I played more or less automatically. Big Logan, on the other hand, seemed to remain quite fresh. Despite the language bar, he seemed to get on the best of terms with those he played with, laughing and joking, so that it was difficult to realize that we were in imminent danger of our lives. In fact, the atmosphere became so friendly that, with the sound of Big Logan's voice booming in my ears, I found it difficult to believe in my drowsy state that I was not back in the pub at Cadgwith.

By midday the air was beginning to get pretty bad and most of us lay down and tried to sleep. Throughout the whole time we were submerged the engineers were working on the port electric motor. Twice it was started up, but each time there was an awful clanking sound. By lunch-time they had given it up, and in the afternoon they also turned in.

The only man who did not seem to sleep at all was the commander. I did not like him. He was the personification of the effects of Nazism upon the youth of Germany. He was cold-blooded, brutal and very ready to sneer. But he was efficient. He could not have been more than about twenty-five, yet his men had complete confidence in him. His coolness when actually in action had the quality of a machine, and I could not help thinking that if the German army were officered by a sufficiency of young men of his calibre it must be a very powerful machine.

But like so many Germans, especially those of Prussian stock, he lacked any understanding of the importance of psychology. He formed his opinion of men and expected them to act thereafter according to a formula. As far as the men under his command were concerned this seemed to work out well—he knew how each one would react in given circumstances. But like so many Germans he had no understanding of the English. Whether we are a much more complex race than the Germans I do not know—perhaps we are. At any rate, I had several verbal clashes with him, for when I told him I was a journalist he began to question me about the reasons Britain had entered into the war. He simply could not understand that we had entered purely and simply because we hated the precepts of Nazism and refused to live indefinitely under the threat of aggression. He spoke sneeringly of imperialistic aims and honestly believed that the whole thing had been engineered by Churchill and Eden.

As regards myself, too, he revealed himself as having not the slightest understanding of the complex psychological reactions that go on in the mind of a man accustomed to living an entirely individualistic life. Because I had been terrified when the action with the torpedo boat had been in progress, he thought I was a coward. And the more he implied that I was a coward, the more determined he made me to prove, as opportunity offered, that I was not a coward.

We remained on the bottom until shortly after midnight. By the time the order was given to blow the tanks, the atmosphere was so thick that it was really painful to breathe. Certainly by then I was cured of any fear of being cooped up in an air-tight vessel. Haldane is perfectly right. You gradually reach a condition in which your senses become so dulled that the prospect of death is by no means unpleasant.

We stopped at periscope depth. The commander reported all clear and at long last we rose to the surface. The conning tower hatch was thrown back and a sudden waft of cool air entered the submarine. I never realized till then how lovely it was to actually feel yourself breathing good life-giving air. Each man was allowed a few minutes out on the conning tower platform and I don't think I have ever enjoyed a few minutes' fresh sea air so much. The submarine was travelling at about 8 knots with her decks awash and the water creaming up white over the bows. It was a fine sight to see the vague outline of her slipping steadily through the long Atlantic swell. The night was cloudy, but there was a faint luminosity from the moon.

'We're travelling due west,' Logan whispered.

'How do you know?' I asked.

'The moon, for one thing,' he said.

'What are they going west for?' I asked. 'Surely with a fractured propeller shaft and one of the motors out of action they'll have to return to Germany for repairs?'

'They wouldn't stand much chance of getting through the Straits now that they can't travel under water. Maybe they're going to try and get round the north of Scotland. Or perhaps they have a base in Spain or somewhere like that.'

Our guards, who had kept very close to us in case we attempted to jump into the sea, indicated that our spell of fresh air was over. With the boat rolling heavily, I found the descent of the conning tower ladder something of a feat. We went back to the bunks that had been allotted to us, and for the first time since we had come on board I really slept. I think it was the drone of the engine that did it. The incessant rhythmic throbbing lulled my senses.

When I woke up the engine had stopped. There was considerable activity for'ard. I leant out over the edge of my bunk and peered into the one below where Logan lay. 'What's happened?' I asked.

'I don't know,' he replied. And then in a whisper, he added, 'I reckon we're not far off the North Cornish coast.'

'How do you know?' I asked.

For answer he moved his arm so that I could see he held in the palm of his hand a big silver watch that he always carried in his trouser pocket. It was turned face downward and the flap at the back was open revealing a luminous compass. 'It's now just after four,' he said. 'We moved off from Cadgwith shortly after midnight. Then for nearly two hours our course was practically due west. At two-twenty we bore away to the north—presumably rounding Land's End. By three-fifteen our course was practically north nor'east. We hove-to about five minutes ago.'

'What's the idea, do you think?' I asked. 'Perhaps the commander is passing on the information he received to another boat?'

Logan did not reply, but turned his watch the right way up. The flap at the back closed with a snap. I looked up to find that our guard had risen from his seat on a bunk a little way down the gangway and was watching us warily. The conning tower hatch was still open. If we could rush the guard, get hold of his revolver and reach the controls of the tanks we might be able to submerge the U-boat. Death would come quickly with the conning tower hatch open. But even as I pondered the idea, trying to remember all the controls I had seen being used, there came the sound of feet on the deck plates above our heads and the members of the crew who had been up above began to tumble in through the conning tower hatch. The commander was last down and the hatch closed with a bang. I cursed myself for not having thought of the scheme sooner.

The order was given to submerge and the inrush of water into the tanks was plainly audible. There was a grating noise for'ard that I did not quite understand and the U-boat slowly submerged. Then there was silence. The commander, who had now left the conning tower, picked up an earphone that hung from a hook in the control room and began speaking into it. His voice was subdued, but I caught the words 'motors' and 'fixed.' Almost immediately the grating sound was resumed.

'We're facing sou'east,' Logan whispered.

'Then if you've worked out our bearings right,' I said, 'we are facing in to the coast.'

He nodded.

Twice the submarine seemed to bump the bed of the sea. I became convinced that we were moving forward, though the motors were silent. There was suddenly a horrible grating sound against the hull just behind our bunks, then another bump and the movement of the boat ceased. The tanks were then blown and we rose slightly.

The commander put down the earphone and moved out into the gangway. 'All right, boys,' he said, 'we've arrived.'

The burst of cheering that followed this announcement was almost deafening in that enclosed space. The men came hurrying from their stations, pushing past our guard in a sort of mad race for the conning tower. In a few seconds, it seemed, the boat was empty. Our guard motioned us forward with his revolver. We scrambled out of our bunks and went along the gangway and up through the conning tower.

I cannot describe my amazement as I came out on to the bridge of the U-boat. I had presumed that we had been brought alongside a ship. Several ideas had occurred to me. I knew that supply ships were essential if repeated and hazardous returns to bases were to be avoided and I thought it possible that the Germans had produced some sort of vessel with a false bottom into which the submarine rose. That, I felt, would account for the fact that we had had to submerge first. What in fact I found was something much more sensational.

3

The Gestapo

The U-boat was lying in a colossal cave. From end to end this cave was nearly a hundred yards long. The width, however, was only about forty or fifty feet. The roof, which was arched like a huge tunnel and about forty feet high, was strengthened by huge steel girders. The whole place was lit by brilliant arc lights and echoed to the hum of giant machinery. I know it must sound fantastic. I was myself utterly astonished when I saw it. The U-boat commander realized this, as he stood beside me on the bridge, and there was a sort of smug satisfaction in the way he said, 'The world has yet to understand—and the English in particular—that Germany does not go to war unprepared. Already we are sweeping your shipping from the high seas. Your papers will be reassuring your people that Germany cannot do this for long as her submarines will have to return to Germany for munitions and supplies. This is the answer. It is a complete naval submarine base. We even have our own foundry.'

As he spoke my eyes took in the whole scene. The crew of the U-boat, some sixty men in all, were crowding the deck for'ard. Right at the bows three men were working to cast off a big cylindrical buoy to which the submarine was moored. The buoy itself was attached to a big chain which ran round a powerful-looking donkey-engine and dropped back into the water. I gathered that it was by this chain that the submarine had been dragged through the underwater entrance and guided to the surface.

'You'd be in an awkward fix if the British secret service

discovered your hide-out,' I said. 'With only that one exit you'd be caught like rats in a trap.'

He laughed. 'Strange to say, that thought had already occurred to us.' He took a step towards me. 'And don't think you're going to be the little hero that takes word to the authorities. Or you either,' he added, swinging round on Logan. 'You'll earn your keep with hard work and you'll not leave here alive till Germany has won the war.'

'Then it looks as though we're doomed to die here,' said Logan with a twinkle in his eyes.

The muscles on the back of the commander's neck tightened. I waited for the inevitable. But he thought better of it and went down from the bridge on to the deck.

'I'm afraid you're getting the wrong side of him,' I said.

Logan shrugged his shoulders. 'What's it matter,' he said. 'He's not in charge of this place, and as soon as his ship is repaired he'll put to sea again.'

'Well, at least try and keep on the right side of the man who is in charge,' I said. 'Somehow we've got to get out of here.'

At that moment the cave echoed to the fussy chug-chug of a small boat which appeared from one of the archways leading off the main cave. In several of these archways I could see the dark grey sterns of submarines. The buoy had by now been cast off. A hawser was paid off to the boat, which did service as a diminutive tug. As soon as the hawser had been made fast the boat took the submarine in tow.

At the far end, the cave suddenly widened out into a big semi-circle. Radiating from this semi-circle were no less than seven caves. Each of these was wide enough to take one submarine and leave a reasonably broad dockside. Each cave was numbered. U 34, which was our boat, was taken into No. 5 berth. A number of the men had small boat hooks with which they fended the submarine off the rough-hewn rock sides of the dock. As the conning tower passed the entrance I saw the top of a metre gauge sticking up out of the water, while folded back against the sides of the dock were strong gates. The tide was apparently at the high. When the tide was low, the water could then be drained out of each basin and the gates closed to constitute a dry dock. The ingenuity of the whole place was incredible.

As soon as the submarine had been moored, we were led along the dockside and up a slope to a gallery that ran along the ends of the docks. We turned right, past docks 6 and 7 and up a long sloping ramp that curved to the left. This brought us to the first of two upper galleries. Here were sleeping quarters for hundreds of men, with rest rooms, which included billiard tables and equipment for all sorts of other games. There were also kitchens and lavatories, and the whole place was air-conditioned and kept free from the damp, that was so noticeable in the galleries at dock level, by means of double doors. The walls, floors and ceilings of these galleries were all cemented so that, though here and there trickles of moisture were to be seen, they were in general remarkably dry.

The crew of the submarine were each allotted a little cubicle which contained a camp bed. Logan and I were handed over to the watch. This was in reality a guard. We were taken to the upper level galleries and into the guard-room where we were introduced to a little man in civilian clothes who smoked endless cigarettes. He had a square head, a rather heavy jowl and little blue eyes placed too close together. He was quite pleasant to us, but I did not like him. Later, I discovered that he was a member of the Gestapo. Apparently even in the submarine service the Nazis do not trust their men, for there were four agents at this base, and I learned later that in each submarine there was always one man in the pay of the Gestapo. The four men at the base, though they were ostensibly there to deal with any prisoners like ourselves that were brought in, divided the day into eight-hour watches, and were in fact the watchdogs of the base, wielding practically unlimited power. I was to observe this power later to our disadvantage.

A few routine questions were put to us, and then we were marched down to the dock-level gallery. We turned off this opposite No. 6 dock into what I believe miners would call a cross-cut. Here several small caves had been hollowed out of the rock and fitted with steel grilles across the entrance. We were both put into one of these. I had more immediate needs than sleep, but as I turned to explain the matter, the grille clanged to, the key grated in the lock and the guard marched off.

The only furniture in the cells was two camp beds with three blankets at the foot of each. I wondered how long the blankets had been there, for the rock floor sparkled with water and the place was chill with damp. The naked electric light bulb in the gallery outside remained on and though it was manifestly absurd that there could be any movement of air, a sort of chill draught rose from the docks where the U-boats lay. The sloping tunnel leading down to No. 6 dock was just visible from the corner of the cell.

I got little sleep that night. I suppose it was past five by the time we were under our blankets. But the unfamiliarity of the place combined with the chill and glare of the light to keep me awake. When at last I did get off to sleep it was to be woken up almost immediately by the clatter of electric welders and the roar and bustle of what sounded like a huge steelworks, for every sound was magnified a hundredfold by the caves and galleries. Sounds mingled so extraordinarily that, except for the welders, I could not identify a single noise. Every sound was made hollow and reverberating by the echo, so that it was as though it were being amplified by an old-fashioned loudspeaker with the tone control set to pick out the drums.

I looked at my watch. It was nine-thirty. Logan, his feet sticking out over the bottom of the bed, was sound asleep. Above the general roar I could just hear the snoring intake of his breath. I lay half awake for some time in that un-comfortable state of reluctance to get up that is induced by an insufficiency of bedclothes. I felt chilled to the bone, yet I had not the strength of will to climb out from beneath my inadequate covering.

At ten o'clock sharp a guard of three men appeared—a petty officer and two ratings. They were equipped with side arms and revolvers. We were marched to the washrooms. But though we were allowed to wash, we were not given any razors, and even after a thorough clean-up I could hardly recognize my own features in the glass. My rather long face was rounded by the beginnings of quite a healthy-looking beard. My eyes were sunken and red-rimmed. In fact, I looked a proper ruffian. I said so to Logan. 'That's nothing,' he replied with a bitter laugh. 'You wait till these bastards have been at you for a week. If the naval authorities here had control of the prisoners it wouldn't be so bad. But you're in the hands of the Gestapo. We're going to have a helluva time.'

He was right, of course—I knew that. But I felt he might have been a little more optimistic. As soon as we had completed our toilet, we were marched off to the guard-room, where we were introduced to another Gestapo agent who was presumably on the day turn. He was a little man with a large head and a sharp face. I liked him no better than the first. He picked up a green-coloured form from his desk, glanced through it and then led us down a narrow gallery that led off the guard-room and into the office of the commandant of the base. This was Commodore Thepe. He was a short thick-set man with greying hair and a fine head. He impressed me quite favourably and I recalled Big Logan's words in the washroom.

The Gestapo man conferred with the commodore for a time in low tones while we stood between our guards at the door. At length the commodore ordered us to approach his desk. 'You know the Cornish coast—is that so?' he asked Logan. He had a quiet precise way of speaking, but his English was not as good as that of the U-boat commander.

Logan nodded, but said nothing.

'We are in possession of charts detailing all coastal information,' he went on. 'We have not, on the contrary, the fullest information about the rock formation and currents close in to the shore. This we require and you can give it to us, yes?'

Logan shook his head slowly. He had a puzzled look, rather like a dog that has been refused a bone. 'I don't know,' he said.

'You don't know? Why?' The commodore glanced at the form before him and then at Logan. 'You are a fisherman, yes?'

Logan was still looking puzzled. 'Yes,' he said hesitantly. 'I believe so—I don't know.' I glanced at him, wondering what had come over him. I thought at first he was playing some deep game. But he had his hand to his head and he was rubbing his eyes as though he had just been woken from a deep sleep.

The commodore looked at him closely. 'You are a prisoner. You understand that?'

Logan nodded. 'Yes, your honour.'

'As a prisoner you must answer questions.' The commodore spoke kindly as though to a child.

'Yes.'

'Then come over here.' The commodore led him over to a glass-topped cabinet in the corner. Beneath the glass was a chart. He slid this out and replaced it with one of the West Cornish coast from the files which filled the cabinet. 'Here is Cadgwith,' said the commodore, indicating a point on the map with his finger. 'Now, are all the submerged rocks charted?'

Logan did not answer, but just stood staring at the chart in a dazed kind of way.

'Are they or are they not?' demanded the commodore, getting impatient.

'They may be,' murmured Logan, lapsing into the slurred syllables of the Cornish dialect.

'Answer the Commodore's question,' ordered the Gestapo man, coming up behind Logan. He had a sharp penetrating voice and spoke English fluently.

Logan looked round furtively, like a trapped beast. 'I can't,' he said. And for a moment I thought he was going to burst into tears, his face was so puckered.

'Explain yourself,' snapped the Gestapo man.

'I—I just can't. That's all. I don't remember.' And Logan suddenly turned and went blindly towards the door like a child in a panic. His breath was coming in great sobs as he passed me and I could see the tears running down into his beard. To see a grown man crying is always rather pitiful. But to see Logan crying was so unexpected that it shocked me profoundly.

The guards turned him back and for a moment he staggered round in a circle. Then he stood still, his face buried in his hands. His sobs gradually lessened.

I saw that both the commodore and the Gestapo agent were puzzled. Well they might be. I was puzzled enough myself. They talked together for a moment in low tones, and then the commodore turned to Logan and said, 'Come here.'

Logan approached the desk at which the commodore had resumed his seat. When he had reached it the commodore said not unkindly, 'I fear you have had an uncomfortable time on the submarine. I am sorry. But this information I require urgently. Either you take hold of yourself or else we shall be forced to make you talk. Is that chart correct for your area?'

Logan's great fist descended with a crash on the desk. 'Don't keep asking me questions,' he roared, and his voice was almost unrecognizable it was so high-pitched and hysterical. 'Can't you see I don't remember. I don't remember anything. My mind is blank. It's horrible.'

I don't think I have ever seen two men more surprised

than those Germans. Until that moment I think they had regarded Logan as either a half-wit or a prisoner bent on playing them up.

Logan looked at them with what can only be described as compassion. There was something extraordinarily animal-like about him. 'I'm sorry,' he said. 'I have frightened you. I didn't mean to. It was just—just that I didn't remember anything. I was afraid.' His hands fluttering uncertainly were surprisingly expressive.

The commodore glanced at me then. 'What is the matter with your friend?' he asked.

I had to admit that I did not know. 'He seemed all right in the submarine,' I said. 'But last night he became rather morose.' Then suddenly I remembered. 'When we were captured,' I said, 'he was clubbed with the butt of a revolver. That may be the trouble. Later, in the submarine, he got a bit excited.'

The commodore pondered this information for a moment. Then he ordered one of the guard to go and fetch the U-boat commander and the doctor.

The doctor was the first to arrive. He examined Logan's head and reported that, though the scalp was cut and rather swollen, there were no signs of any fracture. Whether or not Logan was suffering from concussion he would not say. He thought it unlikely, but pointed out that it was impossible to be sure.

The U-boat commander, when he arrived, testified to the fact that Logan had had a severe blow from the butt end of a revolver and to the fact that, though he had seemed to have all his wits about him when in the submarine, he had at the same time behaved as though he were a little unbalanced. He explained how Logan had roared with laughter when he had been asked for information that would have saved the U-boat from disaster, but he made no mention of that part of the episode in which he had been knocked down.

In the end, we were returned to our cell. As we went out I

heard the commodore giving instructions to the doctor to keep an eye on Logan. As soon as we were alone I said, 'Look here, Logan, are you playing them up or are you really ill?'

He looked at me apathetically.

'Is this some deep game you're playing?' I persisted.

'Would you call it a game if your mind were a complete blank and you were fighting all the time to remember things?' he asked.

Even then I could not believe that he had really lost his memory. 'You seemed all right this morning,' I said.

'Maybe,' he said, as he lay down on his bed. 'It wasn't until they began questioning me that I realized what had happened.'

But it was not until I had seen him refuse his lunch, his tea and his supper that I really began to regard the matter as serious. Throughout the day he lay on his bed, mostly with his head buried in his arms. Sometimes he groaned as though the effort of trying to remember something were too great. Once or twice he suddenly started to beat the pillow in a frenzy of frustration.

When he refused his supper I asked the guard to leave it with me. Bit by bit I coaxed him to eat it. It was like getting a sick child to eat. When the guard came in for the tray I asked if he could fetch the doctor. He understood the word 'doctor.' By that time I was really worried.

About half an hour later the doctor arrived. Logan was lying face downwards on the bed. But he was not asleep. I explained that I was worried because he had refused his food and seemed so abjectly unhappy. Fortunately the doctor understood English, though he could not speak it very well, so that I was still able to keep up my pretence of not being able to speak German. When I had explained, he told me not to worry. He pointed out that it was quite natural for a man who had lost his memory to be unhappy. 'Would you not veel onhappy?' He spoke very broken English and often had to pause for a word. 'He ees among strangers—a preesoner. He fears what will 'appen to 'im.

And 'e cannot remember what 'e was before. He can remember nothing. Eet ees very sad. You most 'elp 'im. Tell 'im about 'is home, 'is village—perhaps 'e remember later, yes?'

He gave me two sleeping tablets to give Logan in some cocoa he would have sent down. I thanked him. He was a kindly man. As he left he pulled a packet of cigarettes from the pocket of his mess jacket. 'These may 'elp,' he said. The packet was nearly full.

Later two steaming cups of very excellent-smelling cocoa arrived. As the man who had brought it placed it on the floor between our beds the guard outside sprang to attention. A tall slim rather elegant man appeared at the entrance to our cell. He was quite obviously a member of the Prussian officer class, the type that would have worn a monocle in the days of the Kaiser. 'What's this?' he barked in German, indicating the cups of cocoa.

The man who had brought them explained that the doctor had ordered them to be sent down to the prisoners. He dismissed the man and turned his attention to us. 'Stand up!' He spoke a thick guttural English. I got to my feet. But Logan remained lying full length on the bed. 'Stand up, do you hear!' he thundered. Then, as Logan made no move, he drew the bayonet of the guard standing beside him and stepping deliberately on to the tray containing the cups of cocoa, dug the point of the bayonet sharply into Logan's buttocks. I saw the pleasure that act gave him mirrored in his little grey eyes.

Logan jumped to his feet with a cry. I feared for a moment that he would strike the man, and I could see by the look on the other man's face that he was hoping he would. Then as Logan stood sullenly in front of him, he said, 'So you have lost your memory?' There was no attempt to veil the sneer.

Logan said nothing. He looked very unhappy.

'Well, we'll soon get it back for you,' the other continued. 'Tomorrow you'll go to work—both of you. We'll soon sweat this insolence out of you.'

I said, 'The man is ill.'

He swung round on me. 'Speak when you're spoken to.' He turned to the man who had accompanied him. It was the little Gestapo agent who had taken us in to see the commodore that morning. 'Put them to work on the hull of U 39 tomorrow,' he said in German. As he moved to go, he turned to me and said, 'I should advise you to see that your friend finds his memory.'

I said nothing, but my eyes fell to the two cups of cocoa now lying on their sides, the cocoa still steaming as it mingled with the water on the floor. I knew it was no use asking for more. The grille clanged to.

'Who was he?' asked Logan dully.

'Senior agent for the Gestapo at the base, I should imagine,' I said.

'What is the Gestapo?' he asked.

I was puzzled. 'You understood what the Gestapo was earlier today,' I said. But there is no accounting for the effect of loss of memory upon a man's brain. 'Never mind,' I said. 'The doctor has given me two sleeping tablets for you. They'll help you to remember things. Don't worry about the Gestapo.' I got him to lie down again and then I collected a sufficiency of water in the least broken of the two cups from a little trickle that ran down the wall at the head of my bed. I crushed the tablets into this and gave it to him. He drank it without question like a child. 'The doctor gave us something else, too,' I said, and showed him the packet of cigarettes. I gave him one and he smiled happily. Then I found that we had no matches. Our clothes had been taken from us together with all the possessions in their pockets, and we had been issued with a pair of coarse dungarees each.

I went to the grille and attracted the attention of the guard. I indicated by signs that I wanted a match. There were two men on guard and they both shook their heads. '*Verbotten*,' said one. I nodded, but pointed to my companion. 'He is ill,' I said. 'It would help him.' They did not speak English, but they seemed to understand, for after glancing hurriedly up and down the gallery one of them passed me a box of Swedish matches with the drawing of a sailing ship on it through the bars.

I lit our cigarettes. As I passed the matches back to the guard I asked who the officer was. He understood the word 'officer.' 'Herr Fulke?' he asked. '*Er ist in der Geheimen Staatspolizei.*' Having said this he turned away. He did not wish to talk. I went back and got into bed. I smoked my cigarette slowly and with great relish and watched a tiny fresh-water shrimp slip slowly down the wall in a little rivulet of water. The guard was changed at nine. By that time Logan was fast asleep. I tucked the bedclothes round him and went back to my own bed, drawing the blankets right over my head in order to keep out the light. It was a long time before I could get to sleep. I was not accustomed to sleeping in my clothes and I found the rough blankets very irritating to the skin of my neck. They had a peculiar stuffy smell similar to British army blankets and took me back to my school-days and camp.

And as I lay there listening to the sounds of footsteps and voices from the galleries above, made hollow by the echo and barely distinguishable above the incessant hum of the dynamos, I felt more miserable than I think I had ever felt before. I had that lost feeling that one has as a new boy in a big school. Had Logan been all right, I think I should have been able to keep my spirits up. But in his present state he only contributed to my dejection. It was not only a question of loss of memory. It seemed to me that his brain had been rendered defective. He had become so childlike that I felt responsible for him, and I was fearful of what the Gestapo might do to him if they were not quickly convinced that he was really ill. I was under no delusion as to the sympathy he might expect from these men. I had spoken to too many who had suffered agonies in German concentration camps to be in any doubt as to what we might expect. The only consolation was that neither of us looked in the least like Jews.

The next day we were woken at six and set to work on the hull of U 39, which stood up, stained and dirty, like a stranded fish in the empty dock. I gathered from the conversation of the men working with us that she had docked the night before our own boat after a cruise on the north Atlantic trade routes. This accounted for the fact that her hull was coated thick with sea grass. Our job was to scrape it clean.

Our guard had been changed at three in the morning. It was changed again at nine. The petty officer of this guard was a real slave driver. To give him his due he had probably received instructions to see that we worked at full pressure all the time, but by the way he watched us and yelled at us as soon as we slowed down I knew he enjoyed the job.

Logan seemed to like the work. Perhaps it took his thoughts off the blankness of his mind. At any rate he went steadily forward with the work, never flagging and doing about ten square feet to my four. My muscles were soft with years of sedentary work and I quickly tired. By eleven the guard was making use of a bayonet to keep me at it. But the stab of the point in my buttocks was as nothing to the ache in my arms and back. We were allowed a twenty minute break for lunch at twelve. Then we had to set to again. The sweat streamed off me and my arms got so tired that I could hardly raise them and at the same time hold the scraper in my shaking fingers.

Sheer dogged determination, induced I think more by a desire not to make myself conspicuous rather than by fear, kept me going. But about two hours after lunch I blacked out. Fortunately I was only standing on the lower rungs of the ladder and the fall did not injure me. I came to with an unpleasant sensation of pain in my ribs. I looked up. The hull of the U-boat bulged over me, whilst very far away, it seemed, the petty officer was telling me to get up and at the same time kicking me in the ribs.

Then Logan's huge body came into my line of sight. He stepped down off his ladder and with quiet deliberation knocked the petty officer flying with a terrific punch to the jaw. Then, before the guard had time to do anything, he had climbed back on to his ladder and resumed his work.

I scrambled painfully to my feet. The guard was looking bewildered. Quite a number of men had witnessed the affair and they were making humorous comments to the guard. 'Why don't you call the police?' asked one, and there was a howl of laughter. There was no doubt that Logan had made something of a hit with the men. From their tone I gathered that the petty officer was not popular.

As the petty officer remained quite motionless where the force of Logan's blow had flung him, one of the guard at length announced that he was going for the doctor. Logan continued with his work as if nothing had happened. It was not that he was trying to pretend that he had nothing to do with the business. He seemed completely oblivious to the fact that he had knocked a German petty officer cold. A crowd had gathered on the dockside above us. Everyone seemed to be talking at once and the sound merged into a low roar that almost drowned the roar of machinery. Men were attracted from other docks, and I could see that the crowd was growing every minute because the ones in front had to strain backwards in order to avoid being pushed over the edge of the dock. Some of them had jumped on to the submarine itself in order to see what was happening.

Nobody seemed to think of going to the assistance of the petty officer, so I went over to where he lay crumpled up against the side of the dock in a pool of water. His clothes were already wet through. I felt his heart, fearful that Logan might have killed him. But it was beating faintly and there seemed nothing the matter with him except for the punch on the jaw he had received. In falling against the side of the dock his head seemed to have been protected by his upflung arm.

I made him as comfortable as I could, and by that time the guard had returned with the doctor. The electric arc lights glinted on his pince-nez as he climbed down the steel ladder into the dock.

His examination of the man was brief. 'He's all right,' he said in German, and ordered two men to take him to his bunk. As the petty officer was hauled up to the top of the dock, the doctor turned to me. 'Vat 'appened?' he demanded. I told him. He nodded. 'Your friend vill be in troble,' he said.

A sudden hush fell over the men on the dockside. I looked up. The Gestapo man—Fulke—had arrived. Like shadows the men seemed to melt away. He descended to the bottom of the dock. 'I hear that man—' he indicated Logan—'has knocked down an officer of the guard. Is that right?' He spoke in German, and there was a kind of eagerness in his eyes that it was impossible to mistake. The man was a sadist.

'That is true,' the doctor replied. 'But he did it because——'

'The reason does not interest me,' snapped Fulke. He turned to the guard. 'Take that man to the guard-room. Strap him to the triangle. I'll teach prisoners to knock down officers of the Fuehrer's navy. Get Lodermann. He is to use the steel-cored whip. I will be along in a few minutes. And take this man with you.' He nodded in my direction. 'It will doubtless be instructive for him to see how we maintain discipline.'

The guard saluted and turned away, at the same time indicating that I was to follow him. They took Big Logan from his work and marched him along the dock gallery and up the ramp to the guard-room. I went with them, a horrible empty sickness in the pit of my stomach. Behind me, as I left the dock, I heard the doctor saying, 'You're not going to have that man flogged with a steel-cored whip, surely? He's not well, mentally? Anyway, his action was not unjustified.' There followed a sharp altercation between the two, but I was by then too far away to hear what was said. In that moment I was thankful to know that there was one man in the place with some human understanding.

But I knew it was useless to expect that he would be able to prevent the flogging. The Gestapo's commands were law, and I was convinced that this man Fulke wanted to see Logan flogged. I had heard tales from refugees of floggings in concentration camps with this same steel-cored whip. It cut a man's back to ribbons and he seldom survived the full number of strokes to which he was sentenced. Something seemed to cry out with agony inside me. As I watched them strip Big Logan and tie him to the heavy iron triangle in the guard-room, I think I went through almost as much mental agony as Logan would go through physical agony later. I felt entirely responsible for what had happened, and it was pitiful to see Logan's docility. He did not seem to understand what was happening. Stripped, his terrific physique was even more evident. I felt that if he cared to let himself go, he could have killed every member of the guard with his bare hands, and I longed to call out to him to do so. But what was the use?

A big powerful seaman had taken the steel-cored whip from an oblong box. He had removed his coat and rolled up his sleeves. The bristles on the back of his thick neck gleamed in the electric light. He adjusted the position of the triangle so that the whip, which was short and knotted, would not catch the walls. The guard had been augmented to six men. The little Gestapo man whom we had first met had taken control. There was a deathly stillness in the room as the man with the whip made his dispositions. The clock on the wall ticked monotonously on as we waited for Fulke.

At length he arrived. 'Close the door!' he ordered. Then he crossed the room and took up a position on the other side of the triangle. His narrow face shone with sweat and his eyes had a glassy stare. 'Why did you strike an officer of the guard?' he asked in English.

Logan made no reply. It was as though he had not heard.

Fulke's hand shot out and he slapped Logan across the face. He did it with the back of his hand, so that a gold ring set with diamonds which he wore on his right hand scored Logan's cheek. 'Answer me, you dog!' he shouted.

Logan's face remained completely vacant.

'*Geben Sie ihm eins mit der Peitsche, das wird ihn aufwecken,*' he ordered.

The seaman measured his distance. Involuntarily I closed my eyes. The steel-cored thongs sang through the air and cracked down with a thud. Three red lines immediately showed on Logan's brown back. They broadened and merged together into trickles of blood that ran down his hairy buttocks.

'Now will you answer me? Why did you hit the officer of the guard?'

Still Logan made no reply. In sickening anticipation I waited for the order to give the next stroke. But at that moment the door of the guard-room opened and the commodore came in, accompanied by the doctor.

'Who gave the order for this man to be flogged?' demanded the commodore. There was an ominous ring in his voice that no one could mistake. A sudden feeling of excitement gripped me.

'I did,' replied Fulke, stepping forward to meet the other. 'Do you challenge it?' There was a veiled sneer in the way he put the question. He seemed very sure of his ground.

The commodore's only answer was to order the guard to release Logan from the triangle. Fulke advanced a step. For a moment I thought he was going to hit the commodore. A vein on his temple was throbbing violently. 'He has struck the officer of his guard,' he said. 'He is to be flogged. Order and discipline are to be preserved in this base. Heil Hitler!' He raised his right hand.

The commodore seemed quite unmoved by this display. He

did not answer the Nazi salute. 'I am in command here.' He spoke quietly but firmly. Then to the guard, 'Take that man down.'

'My instructions are that this man be flogged,' Fulke almost shrieked.

The commodore ignored him. 'Take that man down,' he thundered, as the guard hesitated. At that the men jumped to it. In an instant Logan had been released from the triangle.

'You exceed yourself, Herr Commodore.' Fulke was almost beside himself with rage. 'That man is to be flogged. If you persist in your attitude my next report will be most unfavourable. You know what that means?'

The commodore turned and faced Fulke. He was completely unruffled. 'You forget, Herr Fulke—we are now at war,' he said. 'For three months you have bounced around this base, overriding my orders, undermining the morale of my men by your schoolboy ideas of discipline. This is the submarine service, not a Jewish concentration camp. For three months I have borne with you because you had the power to hinder my work. Now we are at war. We have work to do—men's work. No reports, except my own, will leave this base.'

'You will regret your attitude, Herr Commodore,' snarled Fulke.

'I think not.'

'I'll have you removed from your post. I'll have you discharged from the service. You will be sent to a concentration camp. I will see to it that——'

'You will not have the opportunity. In any case, Herr Fulke, you must realize that men with long experience in the services are indispensable in wartime. On the other hand, the Gestapo is not indispensable. For instance, I cannot think of one useful thing that you can do. Doubtless we can teach you to cook. You will report on board U 24 which leaves for the Canary Islands tomorrow. You will replace their cook, who is ill.'

Fulke's hand went to his revolver. The commodore did not hesitate. His fist shot out and laid the Gestapo agent out with a lovely right to the jaw. I do not know how old the commodore was—at least fifty I should have said—but there was plenty of force behind that punch. His hand was raw after it, where the skin had split at the knuckles. 'Guard! Arrest that man!' he ordered. The two nearest men jumped forward. He turned to the other Gestapo agent. 'You are under arrest, Herr Strasser. Disarm him!'

When both men were disarmed, he turned to his orderly. 'Fetch Commander Brisek here! You'll find him in the mess.'

The orderly disappeared. The commodore rubbed his knuckles gently. There was the beginning of a smile on his ruddy face. 'I don't know when I've enjoyed myself so much,' I heard him whisper to the doctor. Aloud he said to the doctor, 'You'll look after the prisoner?' He indicated Logan. 'Have them both transferred to quarters on the other side of this gallery.' He stroked his chin gently, and there was a twinkle in his eye. 'I think we might put Fulke and his friends in the wet cells that he insisted on having constructed. I wonder how they'll take to the U-boat service—do you think they'll be frightened?'

'I have an idea they will,' replied the doctor with no attempt to conceal his smile. 'What I know of psychology prompts me to the view that Fulke at any rate will be very frightened.'

The commodore nodded. 'I will give Varndt instructions to stand no nonsense.'

The door swung open and a naval officer entered, followed by the orderly.

'Ah, Heinrich, I have a little commission for you which I think you will enjoy. I have placed these men'—he indicated the two Gestapo agents—'under protective arrest. Take a guard and arrest the other two.'

'Very good, Herr Commodore.' Commander Brisek marched out with three men of the guard.

The commodore turned and went out of the room, followed by his orderly. The doctor went over to Logan and took him by the arm. As he led him towards the door, he nodded to me. I followed him. He took us to a small but comfortable little cell on the other side of the gallery, almost directly opposite the door of the guard-room. He sent a man for his bag and in a very short while he was easing the pain of the cuts on Logan's back. Almost immediately afterwards our evening meal was brought to us. It was six o'clock.

When the doctor had finished and had left us, I said to Logan, 'Well, thank God for that! I didn't think it would end as comfortably as this. How are you feeling?'

'My back is bloody painful,' he said.

'I'm sorry,' I said. 'But you're lucky to get away with nothing worse.' I felt this was ungracious, so I said, 'Many thanks for doing what you did. I owe it to you that my ribs are still intact. But it was a dangerous thing to do.'

'Ar,' he said, 'but it was a real pleasure.'

I looked at him closely. His eyes were shut and he was grinning happily. There was something very Irish and a little unbalanced about him. I said, 'Well, for God's sake leave me to get out of my own scrapes. If you knock any more officers out you'll be for it.'

'Is that why they were going to whip me?'

'Of course. What did you think?'

'I don't know,' he said. 'I thought it might be their idea of fun.' He turned over so that he was facing the wall. 'Good-night,' he said.

I stared at him. He just did not seem to grasp things. The old alertness was gone. He seemed dull and slow-witted. I put the light out and climbed into my bed. 'Good-night,' I said.

The warmth of the cell and the darkness were wonderfully comforting after the wet cells in the dock gallery. But even so I found it difficult to get to sleep. My brain was too full of thoughts to be still. The fantastic events of the last few hours ran through and through my mind. I had keyed myself up to see Logan whipped to death before my eyes for something that he had done for me. Miraculously he had been saved from that and now he did not seem to realize what had happened. It was pitiful. But gradually the relief of the changed circumstances—no cold damp cell—no Gestapo—lulled me into a state of coma. I kept on seeing Fulke's face, shiny with sweat, as he realized what the commodore's words meant, the loose twist of his normally set lips, his sudden dive for the revolver. In how many sections of the German war machine were service men suddenly throwing off the yoke of the Gestapo? I had seen the relish in the commodore's eyes as he had hit Fulke. Then his words to the doctor—'I don't know when I have enjoyed myself so much.' If the services felt like this towards the watchdogs of the Nazi Party, how did the German people feel? Was there hope in this for a short war, or merely food for thought? Questions, questions, questions—but no answers.

4

U–Boat Base

It was breakfast at seven next morning and then we were set to work on the hull of U 39 again. Logan worked stripped to the waist because his clothes rubbed against the wounds on his back. But though he moved rather stiffly, he worked with the same methodical speed that he had done on the previous day. My own muscles soon lost their stiffness, and I found the work required less effort.

So morning ran into evening and evening into morning again with only the routine of the place to distinguish night from day. We worked a ten-hour day, from seven-thirty in the morning until six in the evening with a half-hour break for lunch. Hull scraping only occurred when a submarine came in from a lengthy cruise. If it were a rush job a whole party of ratings was put on to it with us and it only took a few hours. Otherwise, we had the work to ourselves and it took nearly two days. When there was no hull scraping, we worked in the canteen, washing up, peeling potatoes. Sometimes, when a submarine was due to go out we had to help carry provisions from the store-rooms and load them on to the submarine. Every morning, whatever else we had to do, we cleaned out the latrines, which were of the bucket type.

Now that we were no longer under the control of the Gestapo we had less supervision. So long as we did our job and kept to the times laid down for us, chief of which were to rise at seven in the morning and return to our cell at seven in the evening, there was little fear of trouble. But we remained under a guard. The officer of the day was responsible for us. He was in charge of fatigue parties. Fatigue parties were provided as required by the submarines in the base, so many men being detailed from each boat. No man went on fatigue more than once until every other rating from his own boat had also done his turn. The whole point of the base, so far as the crews of the U-boats were concerned, was to provide the maximum relaxation—a thing that was very difficult to achieve in view of the cramped quarters which were really very little different from quarters in a U-boat. The main trouble, of course, was that the men never saw the light of day in the base. It was all underground, and, with the constant sound of machinery and the queer echoes, the place was apt to get on men's nerves.

These fatigue parties worked on more or less the same basis as we did, though they were free to do what they liked when they came off duty at six. Like ourselves, however, they had to hold themselves ready for duty when a submarine was coming into the base or leaving it. This meant that the fatigue parties were often called out in the middle of the night as it was only during the hours of darkness that the boats could get in or out of the base.

Thus it was that I was present when U 24 left the base. This gave me great joy for it enabled me to watch Fulke's arrival in charge of two guards. Until then I do not think I had ever seen real panic in a man's eyes. He was struggling like a madman and I was certain he would prove quite useless as a cook and be an infernal nuisance to every one on board. The crew lined up to watch him come on board and there were broad grins on their faces. It was plain that the men of the German submarine service had no use for the Gestapo. It is not altogether surprising. Fulke demanded complete and absolute obedience to every petty and arbitrary rule he made. This may be all right in the army and possibly in the big ship navy, but it does not work in submarines.

The submarine service is probably much the same in all countries. It differs from every other branch of the services because of its danger. It is not a question of tradition or the honour of the service. To be of the service is in itself to be a hero. And a hero is above discipline. Throughout the service stress is laid on efficiency—nothing else. It is a question of existence. Each man has in his hands the fate of the whole ship. In these circumstances discipline is automatic. But when they return to base, especially a base like this, the crews want to relax, not to be pestered by petty disciplinary regulations.

And so Fulke was given a warm welcome by the crew of U 24. I don't know what the man had originally been. Some thought he was one of the Munich Putsch crowd. I doubt it. But at any rate, he had apparently been with the Party since 1933 and had wielded for a sufficient length of time the power of life and death to have become completely callous to his victims' feelings. And now he was scared. I heard one man on the dockside say that he had been in the submarine that had brought Fulke to the base. 'He looked pretty scared then,' he said. 'And he'd been drinking heavily before he came on board. He's a coward—no doubt of that.' And he spat. Then in a whisper he added, 'I wouldn't wonder if most of the Gestapo aren't afraid as soon as they get the wrong end of the lash.'

Perhaps they did Fulke an injustice. Perhaps he had second sight. At any rate, U 24 was sunk by a seaplane in the Bay of Biscay two days later.

Before U 24 went out the commodore walked down with her commander, Varndt. Whatever time of the night a submarine left he always accompanied the commander to his boat. It was a ritual. I saw Varndt's face as he went on board. It was set, but cheerful. Before descending the conning tower, he saluted, then waved his hand. They were all the same, these U-boat commanders—their men, too, for that matter. Most of them were young. They knew what they faced. The chances of death at that time were only two-to-one against every time they went out. The odds were short enough. They had responsibilities thrust upon them at which much older men would have blenched in peace-time. Yet they accepted these responsibilities and the danger without question, and with set faces and sublime cheerfulness went out to almost certain death.

Before I had been in the base more than a few days my admiration for the German submarine service was immense. And I was filled with a great sense of depression. These men were mostly young. They faced death and accepted their responsibilities without question. They were the pick of Germany's seamen. And they were being thrown away to fulfil the destinies of a man whose boundless ambition spelt ruin for his country, himself and half the civilized world. More, they were given orders the execution of which brought universal opprobrium upon them and their Service. In the first days of the war, it was in fact for German youth that my soul cried out against that fanatic, who had diagnosed his country's and the world's disease correctly, yet attempted a cure that had been tried before and had been found only to increase the suffering of the masses.

As far as Logan and I were concerned life was not unpleasant. We worked hard, it is true, and the air was not too good despite a system of ventilation. But in the evenings, when we retired to our own quarters, there were German magazines to read. There was a plentiful supply of these available and I would surreptitiously read stories to Logan. He enjoyed this, but though I talked to him endlessly of Cadgwith and South Cornwall, his mind seemed quite blank. He had loved the place. It had been, I think, his only permanent love. Yet he showed no interest in it and never at any time asked me to tell him about it or describe it to him in greater detail. Much of his time he spent fashioning pieces of wood into models of boats with an ordinary table knife. I suppose it was some sort of subconscious manifestation of the life he could no longer remember. No one seemed to object. In fact the doctor encouraged it. He said he thought it might help him to remember. Sometimes Logan would spend hours carving his name on the wooden legs of his camp-bed as though he were afraid of forgetting that, too.

As time went on, we were allowed to mix more and more freely with the men. They took to Logan very quickly. They made fun of him, but he did not seem to mind. His great bulk and terrific strength seemed to fascinate them. And as it became quite obvious that he was not only rather simple, but also quite harmless, they would take him into the mess of an evening and stand him drinks and put him through his tricks. His tricks were largely a matter of strength. He could lift two average size sailors up on to the bar by the seat of their pants. This, and the fact that a very few drinks now seemed to go to his head and make him fuddled and rather amusing, made him popular. Big Logan had become something of a buffoon, and I found the spectacle somehow rather revolting.

Meanwhile, I learned my way about the base. Generally speaking, we had the freedom of the three galleries, but not the docks nor the repair and munition depots. There were grave penalties for entering these other than when ordered to do so. Nevertheless, in the course of my duties I eventually penetrated to even the most remote sections of the base, and gradually I was able to build up a plan of the place in my mind's eye. When I had a complete picture of it clear in my mind, I made a rough plan, and this, with a few comments added later, I have reproduced.

I have always credited the Germans with a greater eye for detail than any other race. But it was not until I had a working knowledge of that U-boat base that I fully understood what the thoroughness of the German mind meant. It was incredible. Later I was to learn that it had taken two years to build and had cost the equivalent of about £5,000,000. Moreover, all equipment, or the raw materials to manufacture the equipment on the spot, had been brought into the base by a submersible barge. I have already explained the dock sections, the long cave into which the submarines rose, the heavy haulage gear and the seven docks radiating off from the slightly wider section of the main cave.

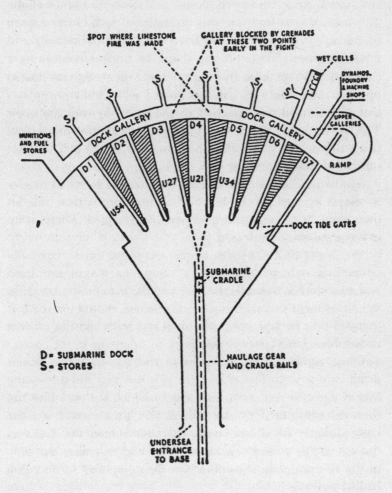

SPOT WHERE LIMESTONE
FIRE WAS MADE

GALLERY BLOCKED BY GRENADES
AT THESE TWO POINTS
EARLY IN THE FIGHT

WET CELLS

DYNAMOS,
FOUNDRY
& MACHINE
SHOPS

DOCK GALLERY

DOCK GALLERY

UPPER
GALLERIES

MUNITIONS
AND FUEL
STORES

D1 D2 D3 D4 D5 D6 D7

RAMP

U54 U27 U21 U34

DOCK TIDE GATES

SUBMARINE
CRADLE

D = SUBMARINE DOCK
S = STORES

HAULAGE GEAR
AND CRADLE RAILS

UNDERSEA
ENTRANCE
TO BASE

I should perhaps explain the haulage gear more thoroughly, though here again I did not discover the details of its working until later. First, no U-boat was allowed to enter the base in any circumstances during the hours of daylight or in moonlight. The haulage gear itself ran out through the underwater mouth of the cave and round a pylon fixed to the bed of the sea about a hundred yards or so off the shore. In suitable conditions, a glass ball of a type used by fishermen for their nets was floated up from the pylon. This ball was coated with mildly phosphorescent paint, and was attached to the pylon by ordinary rope. This in turn was connected electrically with the shore. Any sharp tug on the glass ball—the buoyancy of the ball was not sufficient—started a buzzer in the haulage gear control room. A submarine commander desiring to enter the base had to give in morse by tugs on the ball the number of his boat and his own name. If any unauthorized person attempted to haul it up it was immediately released.

When a U-boat had given the correct signal, a small buoy was released in which there was a telephone. Communication was thus possible between the base and the incoming submarine. When required the main buoy was released, the submarine was coupled to it by a grappling hook at the bows and the U-boat then submerged. Care was necessary to submerge in the correct position, namely at right angles to the shore, or two points south of due west. The reason for this was that the submarine had to come to rest on an iron cradle which ran on a line laid from the cliffs out along the seabed. This, I understand, was the most difficult of all the tasks that confronted the German engineers. The seabed was mostly rock and rails were the only means of preventing the submarine being injured while being hauled into the base.

The base itself had three galleries. The first was at dock level. The wet cells were situated on this level. This gallery ran in a semi-circle round the ends of the submarine docks. Opposite each dock was a tunnel leading down into relatively large caves. These were the store-rooms. They were guarded by steel doors. At each end the gallery cut sharply back from the docks into really big caves strengthened by girders. In the cave near the ramp leading to the upper galleries were the dynamos run by diesel engines, and farther back a complete foundry with electric furnaces. And still farther in were the workshops where there were lathes and machine tools capable of producing every component of a submarine. The big cave at the other end of the curved gallery was a gigantic fuel and munition store. The fuel was in great tanks that resembled the tanks on petrol trucks. There were also stocks of copper, steel ingots, lead, zinc, manganese and other vital materials.

The upper two galleries ran straight, one on top of the other. These were the men's quarters. At a pinch there was accommodation for nearly seven hundred men. The personnel of the base itself numbered over a hundred, while most of the U-boats using the base were of the deep-sea type and had a crew of sixty or more.

These galleries were all cemented to avoid damp and leading off them were big food store-rooms.

The time required to complete the construction of this colossal undertaking and the huge quantities of material which would have had to be brought in through the under-sea entrance made me convinced that Logan's belief that we were on the north coast of Cornwall was incorrect. True, he had appeared to be all right when following the submarine's course with his compass, but in a mental case appearances were, I knew, often deceptive, and I was by no means sure that at that time his mental faculties were quite sound. My own belief was that the direction of the submarine's change of course had been southerly and not northerly, and that, in fact, the base was somewhere on the north Spanish coast.

Though I did not at that time know precisely how long it

had taken to build the base, I knew that it must have been a considerable time. This tied up with the fact that the Spanish civil war began in July, 1936. Germany came into it from the start, and one of the reasons she did this was to obtain air and submarine bases in that country. The more I thought about it the more convinced I became that Logan had not been in a fit mental state to plot a course at the time U 34 was making for the base. And yet he was quite capable of thinking things out for himself. He could do a job of work as well and as thoroughly as any one. It was mainly in his conversation, or rather his lack of it, that he revealed his mental state. He very seldom spoke, and even when asked a direct question would as often as not reply with a non-committal, 'Ar!' I had two conversations with the doctor about him, and found him frankly puzzled. On each occasion, he stressed that he was not a mental specialist. 'I do not onderstand vat ees the matter vith him,' he said on the second occasion.

This depressed me and so did the atmosphere of the base, for as the days passed there was an almost imperceptible change in the spirit of the men. The reason for this was the score boards. At the end of each of the big canteens were large blackboards. On the left hand side were the numbers of all U-boats operating from the base. In all there were seventeen, their numbers ranging from 15 to 62. As and when opportunity offered the boats radioed their sinkings in code to the base. Such communication was often delayed owing to the necessity of surfacing and drying off the aerials before communication could be established. However, experience showed that in general boats reported at least every other day, and there was a standing order that they should endeavour to do this, if possible, in order that the commodore should be able to replace as early as possible boats stationed on particular trade routes which were believed lost.

Information regarding sinkings was chalked up on the boards opposite the number of the submarine responsible. Wherever possible the tonnage as well as the name of the ship was given. One of the first to be marked up was the *Athenia*. This was marked up the day before our arrival at the base. I did not see the boards until after we had been at the base three days. But from the conversation of the men I gathered that they were very jubilant about it. They were not so jubilant, however, when those who understood English and listened in to American broadcasts realized the heavy loss of life and the tone of the American press. Moreover, the attitude of the German High Command towards this sinking was not encouraging. The base was notified of their attitude through the English broadcasts. The base had no wireless transmitter and there was no attempt to keep in direct wireless contact with Germany. Moreover, the base had no seperate wavelength for receiving instructions from Germany. Instructions were given to the base by way of an ingenious code worked into the broadcasts in English. It was only by accident that I learned this—my unrevealed knowledge of German was the cause. All communications to the base were included in announcements about U-boats. How the code worked I do not know, but the idea of it was clever, for no one would look for coded instructions in German propaganda broadcasts.

Whenever the wireless-room orderly entered the canteen to chalk up sinkings there was great excitement among the men at the base, for quite heavy bets were constantly being made either on the basis of the submarines with the greatest tonnage of sinkings or on the basis of the number sunk. But by the end of the first week four boats had not reported a sinking for three days. After ten days, there were seven boats that had not reported for three days or more. Moreover, four days after our arrival at the base, U 47 had come in with her after deck ripped open as a result of being rammed. She was leaking badly and had eight men killed. Three days later, on the Sunday that was, U 21 docked with her bridge twisted to ribbons and her for'ard gun and both A.A. guns wrecked—total killed, twelve, nine wounded.

Including our own boat, U 34, there were three boats in for heavy repairs.

That was the reason for the change of atmosphere. I do not believe that the German naval authorities had reckoned with losses on this scale. Every man in the service knew that the losses in modern warface would be heavy. But seven in two weeks and three badly damaged out of a total of seventeen, was something that brought death very near to every U-boat man. On September 14 the boards were taken down. Every man in the base knew what that meant. Losses were, in the official view, becoming so heavy that they were likely to affect the morale of the men.

It was only then, I think, that I really understood how it was possible for the commodore of the base to take such drastic action against the Gestapo as Commodore Thepe had done. It could never have happened in Kiel or even at a base in the South Atlantic. What had made it possible here was the cramped quarters. The commodore had been thrown into too close contact with Fulke for over three months. Moreover, as in the removed-from-the-world atmosphere of a school, the commodore had come to regard the base as his whole world. Germany and the Gestapo were no longer real to him.

Throughout the day following the removal of the score boards the whole base radiated an atmosphere of tension. And just before U 41 went out, shortly after midnight, I thought the men would refuse to go. They came down to the dock looking haggard and dejected, and some of them seemed definitely mutinous. Once fear gets hold of a man there is no buoyancy in him. But the commander was a tough little bow-legged man, and he came down as cheery as I've ever seen a man who was going to his death. He came down with the commodore full of jokes about what he'd do when he met the British Atlantic fleet. The crew went aboard all grins. A week later U 41 was rammed and sunk by a British destroyer convoying a fleet of tankers from the Gulf of Mexico.

U 41 was the last boat to leave the base for some time. Thereafter, boats were laid up as they came in and the crews told to take a rest. By that I knew some big operation was pending and I remembered the paper that the commander of U 34 had given Logan. The date for the meeting of those units of the British fleet was September 18. It was now September 14. We had three days in which to do something.

This sounds rather as though I had only just remembered this aspect of the affair. That is not strictly true. It had loomed in the back of my mind as something which had to be faced sooner or later. I had certainly not forgotten about it. After all, it was the cause of our presence at the base. But the many little everyday problems of life as a prisoner and the life itself combined to drive it into the background. Only when I saw the U-boats being held back at the base and heard the vague rumours circulating of a big action pending, did I realize that the responsibility for endeavouring to prevent the loss of many British lives rested entirely on my shoulders.

It was up to me to think out some scheme whereby the U-boats could be prevented from leaving the base. And that brought me face to face with another problem—the sacrifice of my own life. I don't suppose I am any more of a coward than the average person. After all, I had been willing to sacrifice my life when on board the U-boat. But it is one thing to accept the line of action decided upon by someone else and quite another to settle down in cold blood deliberately to plot one's own death. But this is what I had to do. I could not imagine any possibility that might achieve my purpose that would not mean my own death and Logan's.

I don't believe I slept at all that night. Interminable hours I lay there in the dark, thinking. I heard the guard changed at three. I was feeling tired but determined to think out a scheme. I wanted to talk the matter over with Logan, but he was snoring peacefully and anyway I was convinced that he would be quite incapable, in his present state, of assisting in the evolution of a workable scheme, and also I feared he might not be discreet. At the same time, I was certain I could count on his help—he did everything I told him like a child.

Not unnaturally my thoughts centred around high explosive, of which there was a big store in the base, if only one could get at it. There seemed, on the face of it, two possible schemes. One was the complete destruction of the base by detonating the munitions store. The other was the blocking of the entrance by means of some sort of explosive charge. Of the two I favoured the latter. It at least gave us a chance of escape, slender though it was. At the same time the submarines were left intact. At the back of my mind I think I had a vague picture of myself presenting the First Lord with half a dozen submarines as my contribution to Britain's war effort. It was the sort of grandiose fantastic vision that revolves in one's brain when one is on the verge of sleep.

I suppose I must have then slept, for the next thing I remember is being woken up by the guard. 'Fatigue!' We tumbled out of bed. I glanced at my watch. It was five o'clock. When we got down to the docks we found that it was the submersible barge that was coming in. It was the first time I had seen it. In appearance it looked like a small tramp steamer—the sort of coastal barges that you see carrying oil fuel up the Thames. She plied between Dublin and Lisbon, calling at the base on each journey and always arriving empty at these two ports. Her papers were faked, I suppose.

We were back in our cell again just before six. As I lay in bed I could hear the rattle of cups in the guard-room. They were always served with coffee at six. I lay awake, thinking. A depth charge would, of course, be the most satisfactory method of blocking the entrance to the base. But there were no depth charges available and anyway I didn't know how to handle them. Another idea was to fire the after torpedo of U 21 which was lying in No. 4 dock. This dock was the centre one of the seven and the submarine's stern would be facing straight down the main cave so that the torpedo would strike that part of the cave which was directly above the under-sea exit. Even if the fall was only slight, it would take a diver some time to clear it away for the cradle to run out smoothly on its rails. The rails themselves might even get bent and have to be relaid.

The only snag was that I knew nothing about torpedoes and felt certain that they were highly complicated. Moreover, the dock gates would have to be open and the submarine floating. At present she was sitting high and dry in a dock that had been emptied of water. There remained only the guns. The after six inch gun of U 21 was in working order. But I was not quite sure what impression a six inch shell would make on the rock. In addition, of course, I had not the faintest idea how it worked or how I could get hold of the ammunition. And then there was the question of my own guard.

The key grated in the lock of our door and a petty officer poked his head in. '*Aufstehen!*' he said. I dressed myself quite automatically, ate my breakfast and started my daily chores with my mind full of the wildest and most fantastic schemes for getting control of the after gun of U 21. I now considered this the only practical means of achieving my aim of blocking the exit. It was now Friday, September 15. The rendezvous was for 1.30 p.m. on Monday, September 18. That meant that the U-boats would leave the base on Sunday night. Between now and Sunday evening I had got to find out how the gun worked and think out all the details of the plan. It was a horrible responsibility, and, because my mind was elsewhere, I was reprimanded several times for slacking.

Throughout the whole of the morning we did service as stevedores, unloading the store barge and piling cases of provisions on trolleys which were then dragged off to the various store-rooms of the base. Some went to the store-room opposite each dock to provision submarines. Others went to the stores in the upper galleries and were for consumption in the base. There were in all about fifty men working on the barge or busy storing the cargo in the various store-rooms.

After lunch, however, I had a bit of luck. We were taken to No. 4 dock where men were working with a mobile automatic drill. We were given shovels and a barrow with which to remove the debris. What was happening was that it had been found necessary to remove the for'ard gun of the U-boat *en bloc* from the deck so that the deck plates, which had been buckled, could be renewed while the gun itself was repaired on the dockside by the workshop engineers. When we arrived, the gun had been unbolted from its mounting, but in order to sling it on to the dockside it was necessary to erect a derrick. One leg of the derrick could be braced against the opposite side of the dock, but it had been found necessary to drill holes to steady the two shorter legs on the dock itself.

The first little pocket took about ten minutes to drill. The granite was extremely hard and splinters kept on flying from the point of the drill. But the other one proved quite simple owing to a fault in the rock and to the appearance of a much softer strata. This, as soon as I began to shovel up the broken chunks, I found to be limestone. It was an interesting discovery for any one who studied geological formations. I looked at the stone closely. It was carboniferous limestone of the type that predominates in North Cornwall from Tintagel to Hartland Point. My immediate interest was in the fact that a fault of carboniferous limestone should occur in rock that was, as far as I had been able to see, entirely igneous. Igneous rock is the oldest of the pre-cambrian group, whereas limestone belongs to the palaezoic group, which occurred much later in the evolution of the world. It suggested that there must have been some movement of the granite formation long after it had been thrown up.

And then another thought occurred to me. Here was a fault of carboniferous limestone, a rock that covers practically the entire north of Cornwall. And the fault was in igneous rock which, though comparatively rare, certainly occurs in the mining districts of Cornwall. Perhaps Logan had been right after all. On the other hand, the north-west corner of Spain has much the same rock formations, with limestone and igneous rock in close proximity. Brittany also has a similar formation. I decided in the end that I was no further forward at all and having, as a matter of interest, traced the fault right back to the main gallery and into the store gallery opposite, widening all the way, I transferred my attention to the gun. Our two guards seemed quite content, after watching over our removal of the debris, to stay and see the gun manoeuvred on to the dockside.

It was swung across by lengthening the long leg of the derrick, and as it was lowered on the ratchet chain it descended slowly on to the dockside only a few feet from me. I had ample opportunity to examine the weapon. But though I could understand the breech mechanism and guess at the handgear for sighting it, I did not see how the thing was fired and I certainly could not imagine how I was to get hold of the necessary shells. The magazine, I knew, was somewhere beneath the gun, but how the lift worked I did not know.

I suddenly remembered that Logan had been on a 'Q' ship in the last war. 'Do you know how these things work?' I asked.

He looked at me quickly. Then he frowned. 'I feel I should,' he said slowly. 'But I don't know.' He shook his head from side to side. He did not seem really interested.

It was up to me to learn for myself. I watched them dismantle the barrel, saw the breech opened and shut and the firing position altered by the handgear, but still I did not see how it was fired. However, if I did not discover the workings of the gun, at least I learned something from the conversation of the men who were working on it. The U 47, which had got so badly damaged by being rammed, had been patched up and was leaving for Germany by way of the Irish Sea and the Hebrides that night. This was only an operating base capable of keeping submarines supplied and effecting light repairs. U 47 had apparently taken such a beating that the engineers considered that nothing short of a general overhaul and refit would make her properly seaworthy. So, patched as well as the base could do it, she was to make a bid for Kiel and the old Germania yard. Apparently she made it, for she was later, I heard, sunk in the South Atlantic. This left only four boats in the base. Among them was our own boat, U 34, now ready for sea again. Two more boats were apparently expected in that night. That made a submarine fleet of six boats, provided the U 21 were ready in time. It was not a pleasant prospect. If they got out it might mean the end of all four of the capital ships in the Atlantic squadron and possibly the loss of some of the Mediterranean squadron at the rendezvous.

At that moment there was a sudden shout of '*Wache!*' Our two guards looked uncertainly at each other. The men at work on the gun paused and listened. The sound of heavy boots on rock echoed down the galleries. Men were running. More men joined them. Doors slammed. The call was repeated—'*Wache!*' Then through the galleries rang the clamour of a bell. 'The emergency alarm!' exclaimed one of the engineers at the gun. And another said, 'Yes, that means action stations.' At that they all went running down the dockside and into the gallery at the end. One of our guards began to follow them. The other hesitated and shouted something, indicating us. Then the one who had been so anxious about us remained whilst the other dashed off to see what had happened.

It was the chance of a lifetime. I looked at Logan, but he seemed quite unconscious of anything unusual. Our guard was watching the gallery at the end of the dock rather than us and his senses were centred on the medley of sounds coming from the upper galleries in an effort to discover what had happened. I heard the ring of rifle butts against rock and rapid shouts of command. The tramp of feet began to resound through the base. I glanced at the guard. He was still watching the end of the dock. Slowly I began to edge away towards the gangway that led on to the submarine. I had almost made it when he caught sight of my movement out of the corner of his eyes and in the same instant his revolver was covering me. '*Ruhe!*'

Was it just luck that Logan was now directly behind him? For one wild moment I thought that Logan was going to lay him out. Then the sound of feet marching in the gallery that ran past the end of our dock drew my eyes. A double file of ratings came marching on to the dock. Others marched on to the farther docks. The guard relaxed. The chance was gone.

The ratings were fully armed and under the command of their officers. They were the crew of U 21. Apparently as soon as the alarm sounds each man has to report with arms outside his quarters. They are then marched to the dock in which their submarine lies and there await instructions. Ten men in each submarine are attached to the base guard as emergency watch. These report to the guard-room immediately on the sounding of the alarm. It is their job to defend the base until the last U-boat has got clear. When all the boats are away, and that may be several hours because of the necessity of waiting for the tide to flood the docks, they have to destroy the base and any submarine that has not been in a fit condition to escape. Then, and then only, are they allowed to surrender. The chances of being alive after the destruction of several hundred tons of high explosive and a large quantity of fuel oil are, of course, not very great.

I could not help wondering at that time why it was necessary in an underground base of this type to have emergency regulations for its defence. Clearly, nothing could attack the base from the sea except by shelling the cliffs above the underwater entrance. It is possible that naval vessels might locate and sink submarines as they left the base, but the U-boats were attached to the buoy on the haulage gear by an automatic coupling that could be released without surfacing. The tricky surface work was only necessary on entering the base. In any case, there was a look-out, the entrance to which led off the cliff side of the upper gallery just near our own cell. This look-out made it possible for U-boat commanders to be notified of any craft in the vicinity when ready to go out.

Presumably, therefore, they feared an attack from the land. And if there were a way of getting into the base from the land-ward side, then there must be a way of getting out. The thought sent a thrill of hope through me. This sudden sense of exultation was followed almost immediately by a mood of complete and utter despair. What chance was there of discovering this bolt-hole of theirs, let alone escaping through it?

I was brought back to a sense of the immediate happenings by the arrival of our other guard. 'We are to take them to their cell,' he said. He was flushed with running and his words came in short gasps.

'What's happened?' demanded the one who had stayed with us.

'I don't know—nothing yet. The emergency alarm went in the guard-room a few minutes ago. Eight men were sent out to reconnoitre. Come on! We're to put these men in their cell and report to the guard-room. The emergency guard has been called out and every one is standing by.'

We were told to march. By this time the dockside was empty. The crew of U 21 had gone to their stations. The tide was at the high and I could hear the gurgle of water as the dock was flooded. The commander and his Number One were standing on the bridge. The boat was not ready for sea, yet they were prepared to take her out and risk it if necessary rather than leave her to be destroyed. It was the gesture of a proud service. As we marched down the gallery and climbed the ramp to the next level our two guards continued their conversation:

First Guard: 'Are we being attacked?'

Second Guard: 'I don't know.'

First Guard: 'Well, what are they doing about it? Who sounded the warning?'

Second Guard: 'They don't know yet. But they've sent out a reconnoitring party.'

First Guard: 'Maybe it's a false alarm.'

Second Guard: 'Maybe.'

First Guard: 'Suppose we're being attacked—what do we do?'

Second Guard: 'Who do you think I am—Commodore Thepe? I don't know.'

First Guard: 'Well, I do. We blow up the exit galleries and then we're caught like rats in a trap. We're marines. We don't belong to the submarine service. But the only chance we'll have of getting out of this base will be by submarine—and the hell of a bloody chance that will be!'

As far as I was concerned the conversation ended there, for we were bundled into our cell and the key turned in the lock. I heard the clatter of the guards' boots as they went into the guard-room opposite. And then an unearthly stillness descended on the place. I had never heard it so silent. All the machinery, even the dynamos, had been stopped. I felt a sense of frustration. Something exciting was happening. Something that might vitally affect our lives. Yet here we were cooped up in a cell with no means of knowing what was taking place. It was complete anti-climax.

I glanced at Logan, who was sitting placidly on his bed. He was listening, too. He sensed I was watching him and he looked up at me. 'What's happening?' he asked. I said I didn't know. I began pacing the cell, but it was so small that I eventually sat down on my bed again. We sat there, listening to the silence, while quarter of an hour slipped by.

I began to imagine things. Somewhere at the back of the base were underground workings. Perhaps even now the guard was fighting an enemy whilst the U-boats slipped out of the base. It did not matter that it was daylight for the exit. How long would it be before they were all clear? Five boats and the barge—that might take between three and four hours. Then what? Would they destroy the base? The silence and my own enforced inactivity began to get on my nerves.

Then suddenly there were voices, the clang of a door and silence again. Ten more minutes passed, and then the sound of the guard-room door being opened and the scuffle of service boots running down the gallery. Within a few minutes came the murmur of many voices and the clatter of boots. Then the gentle soothing hum of the dynamos was resumed. Life at the base was normal again.

'I wonder what all that was about,' I said. I felt almost exhausted by my own curiosity. 'Perhaps it was a false alarm,' I suggested. 'Or just a test.'

Logan made no reply, but I could see him listening intently. I began to talk to him again and then stopped, realizing that it was pointless. I sat on my bed and waited, watching the minutes tick slowly by on my wrist-watch, which I had been allowed to keep. Shortly after four-thirty the grille opened and I just caught a glimpse of the nose and eyes of a man looking in at us before it clanged to again. Then there was the sound of boots on the rock outside and the door of the cell to the right of ours opened and then closed. I could hear the faint murmur of voices, but the rock walls were too thick to distinguish what language was being spoken. The cell door beyond closed with a bang and the grate of a key in the lock. Then the guard-room door slammed to and there was silence again.

Another quarter of an hour passed. Logan was getting more and more restive. Once he tried to pace up and down the cell as I had done, but it was too small for him and he resumed his seat on the bed. I was beginning now to think in terms of mutiny. After all it was not impossible. The men were by no means happy. I remembered the departure of U 41. The commander had only just saved the situation then. The only thing against the possibility of mutiny was the fact that the morale had been better during the past few days—in fact, ever since the word had gone round that something big was pending. It is inactivity more than fear that undermines morale, and now that they had something big to look forward to, I could not quite see a mutiny.

I had just arrived at this conclusion when there came a dull explosion that seemed to shake the very rock out of which the cell was hewn. It was followed almost immediately by a second. And then silence again. Both of us had automatically jumped to our feet. Were they scrapping the U-boats? The thought flashed through my mind. But I knew that it was out of the question. If they had blown up two of the boats the explosions would have been terrific, and they certainly hadn't exploded the munitions store. These explosions were muffled and far away. Perhaps the entrance to the base was being shelled from the sea.

The door of the guard-room opened, footsteps sounded and then the door of the cell to the left of us was opened. There was the murmur of voices. Then the door of the cell was closed and locked, and the footsteps returned once more to the guard-room. Silence again. The tension was making me over-wrought. I forced myself to sit down on the bed again, and I tried desperately to control my excitement. But I could not keep my hands still.

Logan had taken up his stand by the door. I looked up at him. He was standing quite still, his huge body leaning against the door. But for once his face seemed alive and I realized that he was listening, I strained my senses. I could hear nothing. Logan went over to his bed and set his ear to the wall. I did likewise, but I could hear nothing. I went back to my own bed. I found myself wondering how much more of this tension would break Logan's brain completely and transform him into a raving lunatic.

I picked up a magazine and began to read a story. But I could not concentrate. I kept on catching sight of Logan listening at the wall. At length I put the magazine down. 'Can you hear anything?' I asked.

'No, can you?'

As a conversation piece it was not brilliant. I gave it up and for the next five minutes my mind chased the story about the man who asked a lunatic who had his ear to the ground that same question. Someone knocked on the door. I looked up. Logan was standing there, beating a tattoo with his fist on it. Footsteps sounded in the gallery outside. He ceased. But as soon as the guard-room door had shut again, he resumed his knocking.

'Look, suppose I read you a story?' I suggested. I picked up the magazine again.

He did not reply, but stretched out his hand and picked up the spoon from his plate which was still lying on the bed. With this he began to strike the iron bars of the grille. It was getting on my nerves. 'Come and sit down,' I said.

He turned and looked at me, and he was grinning broadly. 'What is the name of your paper?' he asked.

'The *Daily Recorder*,' I said. 'Why?'

But he had begun tapping again, this time much slower. Then he stopped and listened with his head tilted slightly on one side like a dog's. I was getting a little nervous. It would be more than two hours before our evening meal was brought to us and that would probably be my first chance of getting hold of the doctor.

Then suddenly Logan turned to me. 'Here's a pencil,' he said. He drew the half-chewed stub of one out of the pocket of his dungarees and tossed it over to me. 'Put this down on something.' He began tapping again with his spoon. Then he stopped and listened. 'I,' he said, '-c-a-m-e break h-e-r-e break——' He was spelling the words out letter by letter very slowly, sometimes with quite long intervals between each letter. 'W-i-t-h break t-p-l-e-e break.' He tapped with his spoon on the iron grille again. And then went on, 'C-a-n-c-e-l break t-h-r-e-e break m-i-n-e-r-s.'

At this stage it is necessary to digress in order to recount the experiences of Maureen Weston, the novelist, which had such an important bearing on later events. She very kindly offered to allow me to lift *en bloc* the story as she told it in her book *Groundbait for Death*. I should like to take this opportunity of thanking her for her kindness. I have, however, refrained from taking advantage of her offer because I feel that the bare facts as she gives them in her communications to Charles Patterson, news editor of the *Daily Recorder*, together with various other communications which complete the picture, are more suitable to a straightforward narrative of this type. I should state that I am also indebted to the authorities at Scotland Yard for their kind assistance in supplying me with copies of a number of official communications.

Part Two

The Disappearance of
Maureen Weston

Wire from the news editor of the Daily Recorder to Maureen Weston, Sea Breezes, St Mawes, dispatched from Fleet Street at 12.15 p.m. on September 4:

Note story in Telegraph seven two stop Can you cover disappearance Walter Craig query Still a member Recorder staff stop Full details obtainable Cadgwith—Patterson.

The following story appeared under a D head in the Telegraph of September 4, page seven, column two:

U-BOAT ATTEMPTS LANDING

BELIEVED SUNK BY TORPEDO BOAT

From Our Own Correspondent

Somewhere on the Coast of England—Sept. 3: A daring attempt was made this evening to effect a landing from a German U-boat. It is believed that the intention was to land a spy in this country. Thanks to the British Secret Service, however, the U-boat's intention was known before hand and the naval authorities at Falmouth notified.

As a result, a British torpedo boat was waiting for the U-boat. As soon as the U-boat surfaced it put off a boat. The torpedo boat attempted to ram this and at the same time opened fire on the U-boat.

The submarine replied and a smart engagement followed. The boat was not rammed and its crew escaped on to the submarine again. The torpedo boat then fired a torpedo at the U-boat, but failed to register a hit. The U-boat then submerged. The torpedo boat immediately dashed to the spot and dropped depth charges. The first of these brought a quantity of oil to the surface and this encourages the belief that the U-boat was destroyed.

Two men, who were watching for the U-boat from the shore are reported to be missing. One was a local fisherman named Logan and the other, Walter Craig, the well-known dramatic critic.

Wire from Maureen Weston to Charles Patterson of the Daily Recorder dispatched from St Mawes at 2.55 p.m. on September 4:

Busy on new book stop Walter untype involved scrape— Maureen.

Wire from Charles Patterson of the Daily Recorder to Maureen Weston dispatched from Fleet Street at 4.50 p.m. on September 4:

Damn book stop Yard asking questions stop Convinced story stop Cannot spare any one investigate from this end stop Relying on you stop Writing hotel Cadgwith stop Suggest five pound daily retainer expenses plus space— Patterson.

Wire from Maureen Weston to Charles Patterson of the Daily Recorder dispatched from St Mawes at 6.20 p.m. on September 4:

Okay stop God help if wild-goose chase—Maureen.

Letter from Charles Patterson of the Daily Recorder to Maureen Weston at the hotel Cadgwith, dated September 4:

DEAR MAUREEN,

Officers from Scotland Yard questioned me about Walter Craig yesterday morning. There is apparently not the slightest doubt that he and this man Logan have disappeared.

In some respects the story in the *Telegraph* is not quite accurate. For one thing the U-boat was not landing any one, but taking off a man who had been landed the previous night. I gathered from the detectives that Craig met this man shortly after he had been landed and that later he became suspicious. The coastguard is mixed up in it somewhere. It was he who warned the naval authorities at Falmouth. I believe Craig and this fellow Logan lay in wait for the German above the cliffs. The police seem to think that both were captured and taken on board the submarine. There is some doubt as to whether it was destroyed.

The question is—why did the submarine land this German? Who did he contact on shore, and why? It must have been something urgent for them to have taken that risk.

I am sorry to have dragged you out of your book. I tried to get you on the phone in order to explain the situation, but every business in London has moved out to the West Country and it is quite impossible to get a call through. At the moment I dare not spare any one from this end, for though we are running a smaller paper and half the staff is hanging about doing nothing, at any moment a rush of war news may come through. At the same time local men are no good for a job of this sort.

What I am hoping for is a first-class spy story. Good hunting, and very many thanks for helping me out.

Yours sincerely,
CHARLES PATTERSON.

Transcript of a code wire from Detective-inspector Fuller to Superintendent McGlade at Scotland Yard and dispatched from Cadgwith at 4.15 p.m. on September 5. The wire was decoded and sent by special messenger to M.I.5:

Enquiries about disappearances being made by Maureen Weston stop Description height about five-two black hair parted left waved brown eyes slim nails painted young attractive stop Arrived hotel about seven last night in green Hillman ten number FGY 537 stop Has contacted Morgan and now walking over cliffs inspect Carillon stop Keeping contact pending instructions—Fuller.

Transcript of a code wire from Superintendent McGlade to Detective-inspector Fuller at the police station at Lizard Town and sent on by hand to Mr Fuller's lodgings at Mrs Forster Williams', arriving shortly after 7 p.m. on September 5:

Maureen Weston was a reporter on *Daily Recorder* until year ago when retired to St Mawes to write stop Now acting for *Recorder* again stop Editor concerned as to whereabouts of Walter Craig stop Have no power to prevent her conducting own enquiries stop Suggest you help and facilitate disinterest—McGlade.

Typescript of a phone call received by Charles Patterson of the Daily Recorder from Maureen Weston just before 5 p.m. on September 6 and taken down in shorthand by his secretary:

I have been shown the spot where the submarine's boat landed, I have talked to the coastguard and have walked over to Carillon, the cottage inquired for by the man landed from the submarine. But I am no further forward.

However, this much I have got. It gives the background. Walter Craig went out after mackered with a man known locally as Big Logan and came back soaking wet. Big Logan, by the way, is a bit of a character—apparently he is very large and bearded, about forty, tough and fond of the girls. Well, apparently Walter had got pulled into the sea by what he thought was a shark which went for a mackerel he had just hooked. Logan thinks this over and decides it isn't a shark but a submarine. Then, when Walter comes down on the Sunday and begins talking of a fellow he met on the cliffs going home the previous night who had just come in by boat, Logan gets properly suspicious, for his boat was apparently the last one in at Cadgwith. The man Walter met asked the way to a cottage called Carillon on the cliffs above Church Cove.

Logan asks the landlord at the local who the owner of Carillon is. That is as far as they go with the landlord. After that they trot off to the coastguard. I could not get much out of Morgan even though he is Welsh. He is in bed suffering from shock and feeling rather sorry for himself. Apparently the U-boat came very near to sinking the torpedo boat. He says that he is not allowed to say anything about it—not even to get his picture in the papers.

A Mr Fuller introduced himself to me this morning. He seemed to know all about me and why I was in Cadgwith. I began to get suspicious. And when he told me he was from Scotland Yard I was quite certain I had found the master spy. However, it turns out that he is from the Yard and he helps quite a bit. Here's the low down.

It was arranged that Walter and Logan should wait on the cliffs whilst the coastguard and two other fishermen lay in wait just around the headland in Logan's boat. It appears, however, that the coastguard, on thinking the matter over, decided to notify Falmouth, and the naval authorities dispatched a torpedo boat to intercept the submarine. The action was much as the *Telegraph* account describes it. The U-boat is believed damaged, but it is by no means certain that it was destroyed. Fuller told me that the police had found marks on the slopes above the place where the landing was made which indicate a struggle. Their theory is that both Walter and Logan were taken prisoner. Incidentally, the boat made the submarine. It was a collapsible rubber boat and was picked up farther down the coast the next day. On it was painted the letters U 34.

The owner of Carillon was arrested that night. His name is George Cutner. He had been at Carillon just over two years. I gather that he paid frequent visits to London and other places. Nobody down here seems to know much about him. To them he was a foreigner and regarded much as the summer visitors. Any one is a foreigner down here who was not born in the district. He was very fond of fishing, though he seldom went out in a boat. He was often with a rod at a picked spot called the Bass Rock at the extremity of one of the headlands. There was nothing in the least unusual about his appearance. He was about fifty-five, short and rather bald—in fact, much like the retired bank manager he was meant to be. There is a police guard on the cottage and I cannot find out where the man has been removed to. Moreover, friend Fuller seemed to expect me to be satisfied with what he had told me and clear out, so perhaps I had better. I shall take up the search with the agents from whom Cutner purchased Carillon.

I don't know whether you will be able to get a story out of this. However, I will hope to get something really hot in due course. Incidentally, this is the last time I try and get you on the phone. I waited two and a half hours for this call. I'll wire in future.

Cutting from the front page of the September 7 issue of the Daily Recorder:

RECORDER MAN EXPOSES

GERMAN SPY

AND BECOMES FIRST BRITISH

WAR CAPTIVE

NOW PRISONER ON BOARD DAMAGED
U-BOAT

Walter Craig, the *Recorder's* theatre critic, is the man responsible for the exposure of the first German spy to be captured since the outbreak of war. His action has cost him his freedom and possibly his life. He is now a captive on board a German U-boat, which is known to have been damaged and may well have been destroyed.

The spy was posing as a retired bank manager at a little coastal village. For reasons of national importance names and localities cannot be given. His capture was the result of a remarkable piece of deductive work on the part of Walter Craig.

Here is the story as told by one of his colleagues who went down to the place where he had disappeared in an endeavour to discover whether he was alive or dead.

Every detail of Maureen Weston's story that could be got past the Censor was included in this splash. The story was taken up by the evening papers and caused something of a sensation in the Street.

A cutting from the Daily Recorder of Friday, September 8. It appeared in the form of a box on the front page and was based on nothing more hopeful than a wire dispatched from Penzance at 4.45 p.m. the previous day and reading:

113

Agents not very helpful but looking around— Maureen.

The box read as follows:

RECORDER SPY HUNT

Following Walter Craig's brilliant exposure of the first German spy to be captured since the beginning of the war, the *Daily Recorder* has sent one of its star reporters to take up the hunt where Walter Craig was forced to lay it down.

The *Daily Recorder* is convinced that Walter Craig's brilliant work opens the way to the exposure of a whole network of German espionage in England. This must not be regarded by readers as being in the nature of a spy scare. It is nothing of the sort. But it would be foolish to imagine that Germany, which has been preparing for this war for over five years, will not have perfected an intelligence system of the greatest efficiency in this country. This will have been facilitated by the influx of refugees into this country since Nazism first began to spread terror in Europe.

This does not mean that you should regard all your neighbours, especially those with foreign names, with suspicion. But you would be wise to remember not to discuss in public the little pieces of information, military and civil, that you glean in the course of your business or through conversation with friends. Remember—Walls have ears. In the meantime the *Daily Recorder* is investigating this menace.

Wire from Maureen Weston to Charles Patterson of the Daily Recorder dispatched from Falmouth at 4.25 p.m. on September 8:

Cutner imprisoned here stop local force succumbed but Cutner unhelpful stop Declares visitor was commander

U-boat and he gave him envelope contents unknown stop Insists he was purely an intermediary stop Discussion with estate agents at Penzance unhelpful—Maureen.

Letter from Maureen Weston at the hotel, Cadgwith, dated September 10 and received by Charles Patterson of the Daily Recorder on the morning of Monday, September 11:

DEAR CHARLIE,

It's not for the recipient of a £5 daily retainer to doubt a news editor's wisdom in continuing it, but I must admit that you don't seem to be getting your money's worth. Needless to say, I'm doing my best, but it doesn't seem to be leading any place. Either I'm no good as an investigator or else Cutner was just what he said he was—an intermediary. The only objection to this theory is that his identity was rather elaborately faked—at least that's my opinion.

I stayed the Friday night at Falmouth and on the Saturday morning received an answer to a wire I had sent to the local paper at Gloucester the previous night. Gloucester was where Cutner was supposed to have been a bank manager and I had asked for full details as to appearance, interests, visits abroad if any and present whereabouts. The description given in the reply tallied with Cutner in every detail. Interests were given as golf and bridge—golf handicap was four! He was a widower and, following his retirement in June, 1936, he had embarked on an extensive tour of Europe. Present whereabouts was given as Carillon, Church Cove, near Lizard Town, Cornwall.

I then presented myself once more at the local police station. But the law had become unpleasantly official overnight. Exit your glamorous investigator, baffled, to meet friend Fuller on the doorstep. He did not seem in the least surprised to see me and frankly admitted that he was responsible for the attitude of the local force. So I weighed in with a few questions: What were the countries visited by Cutner in his European tour? Was Germany one of them? Did he play golf? If so what was the handicap and had they found out whether he really could play? And so on.

When I had finished, Fuller said, 'So you've got that far, have you, Miss Weston.' I said, 'What do you mean—that far?' He said, 'Never mind.' We then discussed the weather and left it at that. He was not inclined to be helpful.

Deductions, my dear Watson—lucky I write detective stories, isn't it?—are as follows. Cutner vanished in Germany. His passport, clothes, and in fact, his whole personality were taken over lock, stock, and barrel by the gentleman now in prison. This gentleman returned, and, with Cutner's background to fall back on if questioned, purchased Carillon from the executors of the deceased Mrs Bloy. This all sounds rather like an excerpt from one of my books, but I am quite convinced that if only I could get this man Cutner on to a golf course I could prove it. The average German isn't very interested in golf and I doubt whether the man would know one end of a club from another.

However, the net result of this was to send me post-haste back to Cadgwith in an attempt to pick up the threads from that end. But nothing doing. The man had few visitors and no one seems to know anything about them. The police have withdrawn from the cottage and last night I went over it. Not a smell. The police will almost certainly have removed anything they thought might be interesting. But I doubt whether Cutner was the man to leave anything about. When I saw him in the cell at Falmouth he struck me as a secret-ive little man. He looked like a bank manager. His whole appearance shrieked figures, routine and a methodical mind.

I doubt whether he ever had an affair in his life. Incredible the sort of people who will go in for intelligence work! There's not an ounce of romance or adventure about him. If he is a master spy, he's a damned dull one. But there you are, that's just the sort of man you want for a spy.

The point I am leading up to is this. I am no further forward on this business than when I started. I don't mean I've discovered nothing. But I have not discovered anything that would lead me to a big spy network or even to suggest that such a network existed. From your point of view I'm a washout, and after this letter I'm quite expecting you to wire me to get back to my book. The only trouble is I've got interested in this business. The way I look at it is this. Presuming my deduction to be right, why did the German Intelligence go to such pains to plant at Cadgwith a man who was to be no more than an intermediary? It doesn't make sense. Any one would have done for the job of intermediary.

Now I have a proposition to put forwared. I continue this investigation and the *Recorder* pays me expenses. I'll chuck it as soon as I realize I'm getting no further. And if I chuck it you'll only be out of pocket to the extent of my expenses. If, on the other hand, I get on to something that is really worth while you can pay me my daily retainer for the period and for whatever you are able to print. Let me know what you think.

Yours,
MAUREEN WESTON.

Wire from Charles Patterson of the Daily Recorder to Maureen Weston at the hotel, Cadgwith, dispatched from Fleet Street at 11.10 a.m. on September 11:

Okay go ahead stop Good luck—Patterson.

*Letter from Maureen Weston at the Red Lion Hotel. Redruth, dated
September 12 and received by Charles Patterson of the Daily Recorder
on the morning of Wednesday, September 13:*

DEAR CHARLIE,

Believe we may be getting somewhere, but God knows
where. Am leaving here early tomorrow for St Just near
Land's End. It's a long shot and can't for the life of me
think why I am feeling suddenly optimistic.

My last letter, if I remember rightly, was written on
Sunday evening at the hotel in Cadgwith. On Monday
morning I ran over to Penzance and had another talk to
the agents who sold Carillon to Cutner. I don't know
whether it was a sort of hunch or just that, having drawn
blank at Church Cove, I turned in desperation to the agents
as the one possible link between Cutner and the others.

The agents were Messrs Gribble, Tolworth and Fickle—
incredible, isn't it? Previously I had only spoken with the
chief clerk. This time I demanded to see the senior partner.
This was Mr Fickle, the other two being dead! He was a
pompous little Scotsman and vera vera careful. The police
had apparently been at him and he was beginning to fear
for his reputation. When I told him that I represented the
Recorder, I feared he was going to throw me out. However,
we played the old game and I said it would look as though
he were concealing something if he was not prepared to
discuss the matter openly with a representative of the press.
In the end he told me everything I wanted to know, and
it wasn't much at that.

Cutner had purchased the cottage on February 2, 1937.
He paid for it with a cheque on the branch at Gloucester
where he had been manager—ergo, if my reasoning is
correct, this makes him a passable forger as well. He had
looked at a number of cottages before choosing Carillon.

Several of these were inland, but Fickle seems to have been left with the impression that what Cutner was really interested in was one on the coast. An interesting point is that he offered him one at Sennen Cove, which was in every way ideal and much more suited to his stated requirements than Carillon, but he turned it down without even bothering to go and look at it. For some reason it had to be in South Cornwall. In all, Cutner spent the better part of a week in Penzance, motoring out daily in various directions to have a look at properties. An entry in the register at the Wheatsheaf Hotel, Penzance, where I stayed the night, shows that he was there from January 27 to February 1, 1937. He instructed his purchase agreement to be sent to his hotel at Torquay. He was resident at that hotel from December 4, 1936, to January 26, 1937, and again from February 2 to February 28, 1937, when he took up his residence at Carillon.

All this is getting nowhere, you'll say. Quite right, but it shows that I'm being thorough. Now here we come to the little sequence of coincidence which is sending me scuttling down to St Just. The hall porter at the Wheatsheaf remembers Mr Cutner. And the reason he remembers him is that he tipped him with a dud ten shilling note. I know what you're going to say. That dud ten shilling note shows, Miss Weston, that your reasoning is all wrong. Cutner was not ingeniously smuggled into this country by Germany. He is just a petty criminal passing dud notes and ready to take on anything, even a little espionage work, to keep himself in funds. But wait a minute. This man paid his bill by cheque, and it was honoured. He paid in two cheques at his Torquay hotel and both were honoured. As far as I can find out this was the one and only dud note that he passed. My conclusion is that it was just one of those things. But it has served my purpose, for to this day the hall porter remembers all about Mr George Cutner. He remembers that he wore brown boots with a dark grey suit and that he kept a big gold watch, which he would frequently consult, in his waistcoat pocket. And that during his stay at the hotel he had a visitor. This visitor was a man of the name of Robertson—short and thick-set, with rimless glasses, heavy cheeks and a way of puffing as he moved as though he were perpetually short of breath.

Using the office of Gribble, Tolworth and Fickle as a poste restante I wired this description to Cutner's Torquay hotel and to Detective-inspector Fuller at the Falmouth police station. The reply from the Torquay hotel was not long delayed. It read—'Man answering description visited Cutner several times stop Name Jones.' I waited at the estate agents for some time, hoping for a reply from Fuller. In the end I gave it up and went along to see the editor of the local paper. Here I drew blank. No one in the office knew any one of the name of either Jones or Robertson who answered to the description. In fact, no one knew any one at all who answered to that description.

So back to the hotel and further talks with the porter. A genuine ten shilling note changes hands—this will be included in expenses—and from the depths of the remote past this worthy individual, who has needless to say the acquisitive nature of the Cornish wrecker well developed, conjures the memory of a telephone call from said Mr Robertson to Cutner when the latter was out. Later Mr Robertson rings through again and as Cutner is still out leaves a message. The message is to the effect that Cutner is to meet him in Redruth that evening. When the porter asks where and at what time, this Robertson says, 'Seven o'clock. He knows where.'

So then I get the car out and start for Redruth. And as the estate agents is on my way I stop off to see whether

Fuller has answered my wire. I should have been warned by the sleek black roadster that is drawn up at the curb. Detective-inspector Fuller is waiting for me inside with a whole heap of questions. How did I get to know about this man? Who had seen him? Where did I get my description from?

'So you recognize the description, do you?' I asked.

And he said, 'Like hell I do. I've been trying to trace this man ever since Cutner was arrested.'

'Well, isn't that a coincidence,' I said, 'I'm trying to trace him too.'

And then we start the questions all over again. But I get the answer to my wire. This fellow Robertson had visited Carillon several times. So I say good afternoon and thank him for being so kind as to come all the way over to Penzance in order to reply to my wire. He thinks I think I've made rather a hit and that makes him very embarrassed. Even so he sticks to the point and keeps on with the questions. We both get rather hot under the collar and in the end he takes himself off to go the round of the hotels and through the whole gamut of investigation that I've just been through, while I go on to Redruth.

And here everything tumbles right into my lap. The editor of the local paper listens to my description and says, 'Sounds like Tubby Wilson. Started up the old Wheal Garth mine and packed up about a year back.' Then he gets down two bound volumes of the paper and after about ten minutes' search produces a photograph of a fat little man standing with feet apart, his thumbs in his waistcoat pockets and a broad grin on his moon-like face. The man has a battered trilby on the back of his head and I can see a faint mark on his waistcoat that looks like a watch chain. The photograph appeared in the issue of March 2, 1937— that is shortly after he had had these meetings with Cutner.

And the reason the photograph is in the paper is that he has just floated a small private company called Cornish Coastal Wilson Mines Ltd. Then in the issue of March 16 of that year appears the announcement of the purchase of the Wheal Garth tin mine near St Just. Eighteen months later the mine closed down. But it evidently had good backing for there was no question of bankruptcy—all the creditors were paid in full and the mine is still the property of this now very nebulous company. Well, that's the low down on Tubby Wilson. By the time you get this letter I shall be on my way to have a look at his mine and talk to people in the neighbourhood of St Just who worked there— that is if friend Tubby is the man I think he is. I obtained two back numbers of the issue in which his photograph appeared. One cutting I have sent to my friend, the hotel porter, with a request to wire me in the morning if he recognizes it as Robertson. The other I am keeping myself for identification purposes. In the meantime I am trying to ferret out Tubby's antecedents and history. The editor of the local paper, a jovial old boy who regards me as something of an *enfante terrible,* is taking me to the local mineowner's club tonight. I threatened to go on my own, but apparently he didn't think that would be quite, quite. In the meantime, could you have someone go along to Bush House and look up Tubby's ancestors? If you have any luck wire me at the St Just post office.

I suggest you keep these interminable reports and publish them under the title of 'Letters of a Special Investigator to her Employer.'

Yours,
SHERLOCK WESTON.

Wire from Maureen Weston to Charles Patterson of the Daily Recorder dispatched from Hayle at 10.50 a.m. on September 13:

Porter corroborates identity stop John Desmond Wilson known in Redruth prior flotation stop Something of rolling stone been prospecting various goldfields also tin Malay stop Writing arrival Saint Just—Maureen.

Wire from Charles Patterson of the Daily Recorder to Maureen Weston at the Post Office, St Just, dispatched from Fleet Street at 11.15 a.m. on September 13:

Born Dusseldorf ninety four naturalized British twenty two stop Keep going—Patterson.

Letter from Maureen Weston, c/o Mrs Davies, Cap View, Pendeen, Cornwall, dated September 13 and received by Charles Patterson of the Daily Recorder on the afternoon of September 14:

DEAR CHARLIE,

I'm feeling a little scared. Your special investigator is going down the mine tomorrow morning, and she's not the least bit keen. This is the most God-awful place. I've never seen these Cornish mining villages before—they're even worse than the Welsh. They're so drab and the coastal scenery is so colourful. Today, for instance, as I pottered around the cliffs looking at the mines, the sea was a brilliant turquoise blue with a white edge where it creamed against the cliffs. It reminded me of the Mediterranean, except that the coast here is much more ragged and deadly looking than anything I have seen before. From this I came back to Pendeen to make inquiries as to who had worked in Wheal Garth, and by comparison this little huddle of grey stone cottages is unbelievably squalid.

However, I have been quite lucky. I am installed in a little cottage half-way between Pendeen and Trewellard and clear of the depressing atmosphere of a mining village.

But there is no opportunity to forget that I am in the mining district of Cornwall. There is open ground on the other side of the road and it is dotted with grass-grown slag heaps, piles of stones which were once miners' houses and ruined chimneys that acted as flues for the ventilation shafts of the mines. This is what I look out on from my bedroom window. And, believe me, when it rained this evening it looked a scene of utter desolation. It is getting dark now and I'm writing this by the light of an oil lamp. A sea mist has come up and the lighthouse at Pendeen Watch is moaning dismally. However, when it's fine it is possible to see right across to the cliffs, and I can just see the top of Cape Cornwall, which I gather is why the cottage is called Cap View. I feed in the kitchen with the family—mother, father, daughter aged seven, and an evacuee, male, aged five. And from the window there you look up the slope of the moors to the huge pyramid heaps of the china clay pits.

So much for the local colour. Now to the result of my labours. First thing I did on arrival was to locate the mine. Refer to your collection of Ward, Lock, and in the West Cornwall volume you will find it given as lying between mines Botallack and Levant, both now defunct. I have had quite an interesting prowl round. There is the remains of what looks like a miniature railway running for the better part of half a mile along the very edge of the cliffs. There is just the cutting left and an occasional wooden sleeper. In fact, but for the wooden sleepers, I should have said it was a water duct, for it is a definite cutting all the way. Maybe what I think are sleepers are old slats of wood that formed the framework for the wooden trough in which the water ran. Whatever it is, I think it once belonged to Wheal Garth. What I take to be the main shaft of the mine is about a hundred yards in from the cliff edge. There's a high stone wall round it that looks fairly recent. I climbed over and had a look down, lying flat on my stomach. There's a sheer drop of about a hundred feet to a lot of old pit props, and there's the sound of water dripping—most unpleasant! The cliffs here are simply pitted with these shafts. Each has its stone wall, but that is the only protection. Others have been filled, some have fallen in, and the scars of diggings and the mounds of old slag heaps are everywhere.

Your acquisitive little Maureen was seen making for the local with several small-sized boulders clasped to her bosom. Some of the stones on the slag heaps are beautifully coloured, but actually what I had got were several pieces of greenish rock flecked with gold. Optimism outran intelligence and I pictured myself opening up Wheal Garth as a gold mine.

At the pub I find a most admirable and intelligent landlord. Note the style of Pepys! I order a gin and lime, dump my little pieces of rock on the bar and ask if the bright stuff is gold. Whereupon my drink is delivered to me with a huge guffaw and a smell of stale beer. 'Aye, that's raight foonny!' he says. He hails from the North in case you hadn't noticed my spelling. 'That's moondic, that is. Arsenic deposit. Ee, we allus gets a laff oot o' t' visitors wi' moondic. They arl think it's gold.' He produced a piece of rock from the back of the bar that shone like solid gold only the look of it was rather more metallic. This was a lovely example of mundic. Then he showed me a piece of what they call mother tin from a new lode that had just been struck at Geevor. The whole village, incidentally, now seems to live on Geevor. It's the only mine for miles around that is still working.

I know what you're muttering to yourself—when is this so-and-so woman coming to the point? Well, here it is.

The landlord recognized the picture of Tubby. As soon as he sees it, he says, 'Ee, 'a knaw 'im raight enoof. That's Toobby Wilson, that is.' Then over a pint of mild and bitter he gives me the low down on the mine.

Wheal Garth is what they call a wet mine, or rather it was in the old days. Its hey-day appears to have been about 1927–28. Tin was around £240 a ton at the time and they were working on a three-foot wide seam of mother tin. Profits of Wheal Garth for 1928 were something like £200,000. This was on a capital of some £60,000, the mine having been bought for a song in 1925. That's the way with these Cornish mines, derelict one year and then some small speculating prospector strikes a seam and a fortune is made. Apparently this seam ran out under the sea. That was why it was a wet mine. It resulted in very bad silicosis. In the words of the landlord, 'Nae boogger laiked t' place.'

Then in November, 1928, the undersea workings collapsed and a whole shift—thirty-two men—were trapped and killed. It was, I understand, one of the worst disasters in the history of Cornish mining. An inquiry was held and it was found that a huge underwater cavern, which ran into the face of the cliff immediately above the galleries leading into the undersea workings, extended much deeper than had been thought. Thus, instead of having, as they thought, some twenty feet of solid rock above the underwater galleries, there had only been some three feet. The cave was known of course to the engineers and divers sent down when the galleries were first cut in 1916. But the sand that filled the bottom of the cave had proved deceptive. Frankly I doubt whether the engineers took full precautions. Owners are notoriously free with the lives of miners, and 1916 was a year in which every effort was being made by the Cornish mines to meet the demands of the war machine. There might be a story in that for you later—How Cornwall is Feeding the Tinplate Industry. As far as I can gather no effort was made by the company that took over in 1925 to check the safety of these galleries. They were in fact safe enough at the time. It was only when they came to widen them in order to lay a small railway and so increase the output of the mine that they collapsed.

You are probably wondering at my preoccupation with the mine rather than with Tubby Wilson. I must admit that when I last wrote you my idea in coming down here was simply to check up on the man and see if I could find out whether any other suspicious persons had contacted him at the mine. What decided me to pay close attention to the mine itself was the talk I heard at the mineowners' club in Redruth last night. Apparently Tubby Wilson and his activities at Wheal Garth had always been something of an enigma to some members. The point to remember is that these boys have been in the business for years. They know how to run a mine. They know what to look for and what to go out for without involving themselves in terrific costs. When Noye, the local editor, collected a few of his particular cronies—big men in the tin business, as he told me—round the bar and explained that I worked for the *Recorder* and wanted information about Wilson, they were only too ready to discuss the business. When Tubby Wilson floated his company and opened up Wheal Garth, the price of tin was falling sharply. And they naturally thought that what he was going to do was drive another shaft and run fresh galleries out to pick up the undersea lode beyond the spot where the old workings had ceased, so by-passing the danger area. The only thing was, they thought his capital insufficient for the job. They told him this, but he throws a wide guy act and says he's got other ideas. Well, these other ideas are apparently to go for the shore end of the lode. Now this is a bum idea and they tell him so. The lode was discovered only about twenty feet from the sea and some thirty feet below sea level. The shoreward end was worked out before ever they started on the undersea section. Moreover, prospecting work was carried out over a wide area at the shoreward end in a fruitless effort to discover the continuation of a lode. The boys at the club told him he'd be throwing his money away if he started looking for that end of the lode. His reply was that he had an idea. Well, his idea was to sink a new shaft about a hundred yards back from the cliffs dead in a line with the cave, then he throws new galleries out until he meets the cave which apparently extends some two hundred yards inland. Then he begins to cast about in a big semi-circle with broad adits running off every few yards into the cave. Then he casts inland in two great drives at each end of his main gallery. Then he runs adits off opposite the ones he has run into the cave. Then he tries a higher level. Then a higher level still. Then he goes bust and the mine closes down.

The boys I spoke to thought he must have spent in all four times the nominal capital of the company. He employed forty men on the job and an engineer who came down from London and didn't know a thing about Cornish tin mining. They think he was nuts. What do you think?

Anyway, that's why I'm fussing over the mine. I'm also interested in this engineer from London—long lean fellow with horn-rimmed spectacles, thinning hair and what is thought to have been the makings of a Scotch accent. The name is Jesse Maclean. See what you can get?

It was the landlord who put me on to Alf Davies. Davies is a Welshman, whatever, and was foreman of the Wheal Garth under Maclean. I thanked him and asked whether it would be possible to have a look over the mine. He said it was closed, but that Alf Davies would be able to tell me all about it.

Davies is a proper little Welsh miner, short and broad, a bundle of muscle and vitality, with false teeth and a sour glum-looking face beaten brown by the wind. But for all his glumness, he's got a sense of humour and smiles some-times. When I asked him after tea this afternoon whether he could take me down Wheal Garth he said, 'Indeed and I'd like to, but look you the mine is closed.' I said there must surely be some way in and offered him a fiver for his trouble—please note for expenses! I saw him hesitate, for he is on the dole now, and then he said, 'Well, if you're so anxious that it's worth that much to you to go down a lousy mine like Wheal Garth I can't stop you. But there's no dependence on the old workings whatever and it's rough going, by damn it is.' I said I didn't mind, so it's all fixed up. In due course I'll let you know what happens. I must admit I haven't the faintest idea what I'm expecting to find. It's just that I'm curious.

Yours,
MAUREEN.

Transcript of code wire from Detective-inspector Fuller to Superintendent McGlade at Scotland Yard, dispatched from Penzance at 3.15 p.m. on September 13:

All information John Desmond Wilson mine owner and gold prospector please stop Formed Cornish Coastal Wilson Mines Ltd April thirty seven—Fuller.

Transcript of a code wire from Superintendent McGlade to Detective-inspector Fuller at police station, Penzance, dispatched at 5.55 p.m. on September 13:

Wilson born Dusseldorf ninety four naturalized British twenty two stop No police record stop *Daily Recorder* made similar inquiries today stop Intelligence officer meeting you in morning—McGlade.

Letter from Maureen Weston posted at Penzance on the evening of September 14 and received by Charles Patterson of the Daily Recorder on the Friday afternoon:

DEAR CHARLIE,

Further to my report of September 13, I have examined the mine and quite frankly the experience was not a pleasant one. For one thing, you've no idea how eerie the place was. It reeked of water and the air was pretty stale. For another, my guide seemed to become rather uneasy when we reached the lower levels. I know that must sound silly—it does to me now I am sitting writing about it in the cosy warmth of my little bedroom. But, believe me, it is unpleasant enough going down a discarded Cornish tin mine without your guide getting scared. Perhaps 'scared' isn't quite the right word. 'Puzzled' might be better—and yet he was more than just puzzled. He was quite confident when we started. After all, it was his mine, so to speak. But there are all sorts of funny noises in those empty galleries. The drip of water echoes and is magnified. There are strange creaking sounds where old props are taking a strain, queer glimpses of pale light where old shafts come down, the sound of falling stones, the weird echo of one's own footsteps going up one gallery and coming back at one down another, and at the lower levels a faint roar as of water falling. I didn't worry much about all these weird sounds until I sensed that Alf was uneasy. Then these sounds became so magnified in my imagination that at times I could have sworn we were being followed and at other times that the roof of the gallery was coming down.

This probably reads rather like the hysterical blathering of a woman who has been thoroughly frightened by her first experience of going down a mine, so I had better begin at the beginning. To start with, I'll go over my conversation with Alf Davies on the previous night in greater detail. When I asked him whether he could take me over the mine and he hesitated at the suggestion of a fiver, he told me one or two things. First, that so far as he knew the mine had not been entered since it had closed down in 1937. Second, that the new main shaft had been blocked at the bottom. Third, that the only possible means of getting into the mine was the way they had got into it when they opened it up in 1937. Fourth, that this entrance meant going through the old workings which were not particularly safe, and that to get into them necessitated climbing down an old half-ruined shaft with the aid of a rope. I must admit the prospect was not exactly encouraging, but I had made up my mind to have a look at the mine, so I put the best face I could on it and said I adored climbing down unsafe shafts on the end of a rope.

Well, we left at eight-thirty this morning equipped with a coil of rope, a pair of electric torches and a packet of sandwiches apiece. Fortunately I had had the sense to bring a pair of old corduroy trousers with me on this assignment of yours so that I looked reasonably business-like. We walked for about a quarter of a mile through the waste of old mine workings opposite the cottage and then went through a gate and crossed a field. Thence through another gate on to the sort of heath that runs to the cliff edge. There were no mine chimneys here, but grass mounds and barrows pointed to old workings, and here and there were the small circular walls that marked a shaft. We struck away to the left along the wall that circled the field, pushing our way through a tangle of briars. We then came to a vague fork in the path and bore right, away from the wall. The ground here was covered with briar and heather—or heath, I never know which.

I don't think I've ever seen such a frighteningly desolate spot. The ground about us was pock-marked with old workings, all overgrown and ruined. Some of the shafts had only pieces of rotting timber across them with a few lumps of rock thrown carelessly on top. One or two we passed were practically unprotected, with ferns growing out of the sides and very wet. Alf told me that the cattle quite often fall down these shafts. 'Quite a good place for a murder,' I said, wondering whether to make this the setting for my next book. But Alf—I'd told him what I did for a living—said, 'Yes, indeed, it is creepy enough, but you would not get away with it.' Apparently as soon as a carcase that has fallen down a shaft begins to rot the birds gather over it in clouds. That was the moment he chose to introduce me to the entrance to the old workings of Wheal Garth and I had an immediate vision of ravens and gulls and choughs wheeling in a monotonous screaming symphony of black and white over our decaying bodies.

A more evil-looking spot than the entrance to those workings I cannot imagine. Out of a tangle of briars rose an old lichen-covered wall that was rapidly disintegrating. It was circular, like all the rest, and about twelve feet in diameter. And when I looked over, it was to peer down into a black wet pit surrounded by ferns and water-weed. 'Do I have to go down that?' I asked. At that he grinned. 'Indeed and ye don't have to, miss, it's your own party.'

I smiled a little weakly. He was right—I didn't have to. Quite frankly I nearly walked out on him. However, I asked him whether he thought it was all right, and he said, 'Yes, indeed, why not?' And he seemed so confident about it and so matter-of-fact that I said nothing when he began looking around for a suitable rock to which he could secure the rope.

By the way, I think I owe you an apology for writing you such long screeds when from your own point of view there is very little news in them. But I am regarding these daily reports to you as a sort of diary, and whatever material you don't use I shall probably incorporate in a book.

Well, he secured the rope to a good-sized rock, clambered over the wall and dropped the other end of it down the shaft. He then asked me whether I thought I was capable of climbing down the rope or if it would be better for him to lower me down. When I discovered that if he lowered me it would necessitate my going down first and waiting at the bottom alone, I decided to risk the climb. The depth of the shaft was apparently only a matter of thirty or forty feet. As he lowered his legs into the shaft he looked up at me and said, 'Don't ye mind about anything else but the rope.' I asked him what he meant and he grinned and quoted, 'Fra' ghoulies and ghosties and long-leggety beasties. I'm not saying there mayn't be a bat or two down here,' he explained. 'Just you remember to hang on to the rope.' Then he caught hold of the rope and disappeared. It was a good start.

I could hear his feet scrabbling against the uneven stone sides of the shaft, and several times stones clattered down into the depths, making a hollow unreal sound. Then the rope went slack and his voice came up the shaft, deep and cavernous. I climbed over the wall and sat down with my legs dangling over the edge of the shaft. And there I remained for what seemed an age. I suppose it was, in fact, only a few seconds, but I thought I should be rooted there for ever. There were large ferns in the shaft and the stone sides were all slimy with water. And there were little noises that I could not recognize.

The feeling I had sitting on top of that shaft was horribly primitive. It's funny. I wouldn't have minded going down a new shaft. In fact, I shouldn't have hesitated. We're quite accustomed to going underground. We do it every day in London. But when the shaft leading underground is shorn of its civilized trappings you suddenly realize that when you descend you will be going *under ground*.

Then Alf's voice came floating up to me again, and I knew it was very little different from the first bathe of the season and that the sooner I got on with it the better. So, before I could change my mind and start panicking again, I had swung my legs over, gripped the rope with my feet and was lowering away. Strange as it may seem, it wasn't as unpleasant as I had expected, chiefly, I imagine, because my whole attention was concentrated on the task of keeping hold of the rope. I thought my arms would never stand it. I couldn't come down gripping the rope with my feet because it swung close to the wall and was apt to rub my nose against the slimy water-weed. I had to let my arms take the strain and brace my feet against the many crevices that I found in the side. There were quite a number of cobwebs and I'm sure that I should have hated it if I'd had a torch. But as soon as I had got about ten feet down it was quite impossible to see a thing except the glaring white circle of daylight at the top, and this gradually diminished in size. Once, I did encounter a bat, but by that time I was too concerned about whether or not I should ever last out till the bottom to worry about it. It fluttered about for a few moments and then settled again. I think it was dark enough for it to see me and avoid me. What I should have done if it had flown in my face I don't know.

Just as I thought my arms would be wrenched from

their sockets, I felt Alf's hand grip me and I stepped down on to the level floor of the shaft. 'Ye ought to come to Wales and do some real climbing,' he said. It was a compliment which I felt I had deserved. I moved my feet and immediately there was a dry rattle. I flashed my torch and stared a little uncomfortably at the skeleton of what I presumed had once been a cow.

Alf switched his torch on and disappeared along a wet stale-smelling tunnel that gradually sloped at a steeper and steeper angle. I followed him. It was rather like exploring a long cave. There was little to show that the walls had been cut by human hands. They were rough and not hewn to any definite shape. Here and there were slight falls that had to be negotiated, sometimes with considerable difficulty, and the floor was irregular and strewn with stones that made it treacherous. In places it was like the bed of a stream. Alf told me that he believed these particular workings dated back more than two centuries. I could well believe it. But the thought that they had stood for that long comforted me. In one part, however, there had been a particularly bad fall and for a time we thought we should not be able to get through. But by removing one or two rocks we were able to crawl under it on our hands and knees. Alf spent some time examining this fall, and when I asked him what he was up to, he said he was just wondering what had caused it.

After about half an hour's very uncomfortable travelling, mostly down a sharp incline, we suddenly struck the level and the roof rose so that we could walk upright. We had reached the more recent workings. My back ached abominably. However, from then onwards the going was much less difficult.

Now this is what I want to impress upon you. The unpleasant part was over. We had left the old workings.

The workings we were in now were quite safe—that is as mines go down this part of the world. Yet we hadn't progressed more than a hundred yards into these new workings before I began to feel uneasy. That sounds daft, I know. But the fact remains that throughout our scramble through the old workings it had seemed rather fun—an adventure. Now I didn't like it.

The reason, I am convinced, was Alf. He was the guide and he had been so assured coming through the old workings that I had complete confidence in him. It was his mine and I felt he ought to know his way about it like his own house. But my reliance on him made me very susceptible to his mood, and I was not slow in sensing what I think was a certain bewilderment—the sort of feeling one has if one is not sure of the way out. Its effect on me was to produce an immediate sense of uneasiness. I became jittery and all the unfamiliar little sounds about me—the drip of water, the rattle of stones and the echo of our movements—became magnified in the stillness.

I didn't get as frightened as all that at once. It was cumulative. It started when we came to a point in the more recent workings where the water that ran down from the old workings, and it was deep enough now to be over our ankles in places, was diverted from what I believe is known as a winze. This is a sharp slope going down from one level to the next, and a little wall of stones had been erected across it and cemented together so that the water continued along the level on which we stood. Alf examined this artificial barrier for a moment in the light of his torch. He even bent down and felt the cement with his hand. Then we splashed on along the level and heard the sound of falling water. It was a faint splashy sound, and suddenly we came to the end of the level.

At this point the gallery was wide enough for us to

walk abreast and I got rather an unpleasant shock when in the light of the torch I saw that the floor level simply vanished. We could hear the splash of water on rock many feet below. There was no ceiling either. In fact the level ran out into an old shaft that was blocked at the top.

I don't know why the discovery that the level just ended in a sheer drop should have upset me so much. I think there must always be something very unpleasant about finding a sheer drop underground. Probably it is the immediate and involuntary feeling that if one had no torch and stumbled on it in the dark one would now be lying at the bottom where the water was splashing. I felt rather foolish really, because quite automatically I had clutched at Alf's arm—and as a one-time Fleet Street woman I pride myself on being tougher than most females. I mean, damn it, one knows quite well that mine shafts are put down and levels cut at various depths.

We retraced our steps and went down the winze into the next level. At the bottom we turned left until we came to what Alf described as a cross-cut. We took this and at the end turned right. By this time I was feeling an uncomfortable desire to cling on to his arm. With all these bewildering turns and the memory of that drop into the old shaft, I was terrified of being separated from him. I remembered all sorts of ghoulish stories about the catacombs of Rome, and pictured myself wandering alone in the place till I either died of starvation or killed myself by falling down a shaft in the dark. It was from this point, I think, that I began to get really frightened of the dark. It seemed to press in on us from every side as though endeavouring to muffle our torches. The air was warm and stale and damp, and the echo of our footsteps had an unpleasant habit of coming back at us down the disused galleries long after we had moved.

Quite often now Alf would pause and listen, with his head cocked on one side. I asked him once whether he was listening for ghosts, thinking of the miners who had been trapped. But he didn't smile. His round craggy face was set and taciturn. Every time we paused we could hear that faint roar, as of an underground waterfall, and the echo of footsteps came whispering back at us. It was then I began to feel that we were being followed. I no longer felt sure it was the echo of our own footsteps. Again I remembered the men who had lost their lives in that disaster ten years ago. We were nearing that section of the mine and I began to see in every shadow the ghost of a dead miner. Once I cried out at my own shadow cast against a wall of rock ahead of me. I tell you, I was really frightened.

By this time we had descended another winze and Alf announced in a whisper that we had reached the lowest level in this section of the mine. And a second later down the gallery behind came the whisper—'the lowest level in this section of the mine'—with the sibilants all magnified. It was uncanny. There was a good deal of timber in this section, not all of it sound. Much of it was green and beginning to rot. Once I stumbled on a piece of rock and clutched at a prop to save myself from falling. The outer surface of the wood crumbled in my hand, all wet and sloppy.

Then we came to the bricked up foot of the new shaft. We bore away to the left along a gallery in which the timber was still grey and sound. The gallery sloped downwards and curved away to the right. Sections of rail still lay along the floor and the roar of distant water was much louder. The sound was peculiar and distorted, more like a hum, as though a rushing cataract were pouring through a narrow gorge. Remembering the disaster, I felt that at any moment we might be overwhelmed by a wall of water, though Alf assured me we were still well above sea level. My nerves were completely gone.

At length the gallery flattened out and branched into three. Alf hesitated, and then took the right-hand branch. The sound of water became even louder. The gallery here was very well built. It was about seven feet wide and the same high, and in places it was cemented to keep out the water. Then suddenly we rounded a bend and came face to face with the most ghastly-looking fall. The whole of the roof had simply caved in and the gallery was blocked by great chunks of rock that looked as though they might have been part of Stonehenge. It suddenly made me realize that it is possible to get trapped in even the soundest-seeming galleries.

Alf played his torch over the debris and at length we turned back and retraced our steps to where the main gallery had branched. We took the next branch, and before we had gone more than forty feet we came up against another huge fall. I began to have a feeling that the whole place must be unsafe. All I wanted to do was to get out of it before it caved in on top of us.

Alf spent even longer examining this fall. But at length he led me back and down the next branch. It was the same thing. Thirty feet or so down the gallery we were stopped by a fall. I guessed then that there must be a serious fault in the whole rock formation at this point. I said as much to Alf, but he only grunted and continued to poke about amongst the debris. Then he began to examine the walls.

At last I could stand it no longer. 'I'm getting out of this,' I said.

He nodded. 'All right, miss,' he said. But he made no move. He simply stood there with his head on one side, listening. Involuntarily I began to listen too. I could hear the hum of the water somewhere beyond the falls and occasionally there was the creak of a pit prop.

I suddenly clutched his arm. 'I can't stand this,' I said. 'What are you listening for? What's the matter with the place?' He seemed a little put out by my questions. 'You're uneasy, aren't you?' I went on. 'I've felt it ever since we left the old workings. For God's sake tell me what it is. Have we lost our way, is somebody following us—what? I don't mind so long as you tell me what it is.'

Then he told me. 'Somebody has been in this mine since it was closed down,' he said. He told me not to be alarmed. Then he said, 'Remember that fall we had to scramble through in the old workings?' I nodded. 'That was what first made me uneasy,' he went on. Then he explained that he thought the fall unnatural. 'Do you suppose it would have been done to discourage people from entering the mine?' he asked. Then he pointed out that the watercourse had been diverted. Normally it would have run through these workings and out beyond into the cave. And what about these falls, he asked. He took my hand and showed me clean-cut flakes on the walls and marks as though the rock had been blackened. 'These falls are not natural,' he said. He spoke fast and excited in his musical Welsh voice. 'The rock has been blasted. Those marks are the marks of dynamite. Someone has blocked off the new workings.' He swung round on me. 'Why is that?' he asked. 'Indeed, and can you tell me why you wanted to come down this mine?'

I explained that I had reason to be suspicious of the last owner. He looked at me with his head on one side. 'Mr Wilson was not a good man,' he said. 'But I did not think him dishonest.'

He took my arm and led me back up the gallery.

'Tomorrow we will come down with two friends of mine. I believe we may be able to find a way through this fall.'

And that is how things stand at the moment. We got out of the mine shortly after one. I felt pretty near exhausted and very dirty. Since then I have had a wash, a meal and a rest. I don't know what to think. I had a hunch that the mine would be worth looking at. Now I've been down it and am informed that someone has tampered with it since it was closed—in fact, that someone has deliberately produced four falls of rock. But we were able to get through the first fall—the one in the old workings. Was that design or inefficiency? Was I mistaken when I had that unpleasant feeling that we were being followed? And the three big falls—what was on the other side? What is that faint roar of water? Alf says it doesn't sound like water. Is somebody drilling? The whole thing is so fantastic. Do you remember Conan Doyle's *Tales of Horror and Mystery*? Well, I feel as though I'm writing the diary in one of his tales of horror that will be found after I am dead and from which others will draw the wildest conjectures. Suppose there is an underground race and they are coming to the surface to conquer us? Stupid! But when you are deep in the bowels of the earth anything seems possible. Quite frankly I'm not looking forward to tomorrow.

Your scared investigator,
MAUREEN.

P.S. Since writing this I have heard rather a peculiar thing. I went down to the local as Alf's guest. They're a tough crowd at Pendeen, but very friendly. I met Alf's pals who are coming on tomorrow's expedition. One's tall and the other's short, and they both look very tough indeed. They're out of work, like Alf. Both worked in Wheal Garth under Maclean. What I wanted to tell you, however, is a curious little story that is drifting around. They are very superstitious in this neighbourhood and apparently there has been talk recently of the miners who were killed in that disaster lying uneasy. They say that the white skull of a dead miner can be seen on dark nights floating in the sea just off Wheal Garth right over the spot where they were trapped.

Now the talk was going on about this when an old boy in the corner of the pub gives tongue and says that his son that keeps a bar over to St Ives told him a fisherman coming back late the other night picked up a glass net float that was bobbing up and down in the water and shining like a little full moon. It was apparently covered with phosphorous. 'That's what you see,' the old man said. 'That flawt were drifting and a phawsphorescent fish rubbed itself against it. The skull of a dead miner!' He laughed.

I thought about this as Alf and I were walking home. 'What do you think?' I asked. He shrugged his shoulders. 'Miners are superstitious folk,' he said. It was a dark night. 'I've got a pair of binoculars in the car,' I said. 'Would you care to walk with me as far as the cliffs?' He agreed, so we fetched the glasses and walked over to the cliffs. Well, it was there all right. At first I could see absolutely nothing. It was so dark that, looking through the glasses, it was as though I had covered the lenses with my hands. And then suddenly I saw a faint little point of light bobbing about like a will-o'-the-wisp. Alf saw it too. It was so faint that is was barely visible. But it was there all right.

Now what do you make of that? I hear there's a boat to be hired at Cape Cornwall. Tomorrow night, if I get back from the mine in time, I'm going out to have a look at the skull of that miner if I can get someone to come with me. Alf was very silent as we walked back. I don't know whether he, too, is superstitious, or if he was just trying to reason things out. I must admit that I don't feel too happy myself. It's easy to be matter-of-fact in a newspaper office and pour verbal ridicule upon country superstitions. But down here there seems a bit more to it. After all, there are thirty-odd men lying dead under the bed of the sea there. I think I'm going to have nightmares tonight. Now I must go out and post this endless screed. I'll report developments tomorrow. I wonder how long it will take us to get through one of those falls?—M. W.

Wire from Charles Patterson of the Daily Recorder to Maureen Weston at Cap View, Pendeen, dispatched from Fleet Street at 3.25 p.m. on Friday, September 15:

Jesse Maclean British now directing mining work of national importance for Supply Ministry stop No police record nothing against him—Patterson.

Wire from Charles Patterson of the Daily Recorder to Maureen Weston at Cap View, Pendeen, dispatched from Fleet Street at 6.10 p.m. on Friday, September 15:

Letter received grand work stop Wire results days operations—Patterson.

Wire from Charles Patterson of the Daily Recorder to Maureen Weston at Cap View, Pendeen, dispatched from Fleet Street at 10.50 a.m. on Saturday, September 16:

Report at once results yesterdays activities—Patterson.

Wire from Charles Patterson of the Daily Recorder to Davies at Cap View, Pendeen, dispatched from Fleet Street at 12.35 p.m. on Saturday, September 16 and carrying with it a reply-paid form:

Please inform whereabouts of Maureen Weston residing with you—Patterson.

Pre-paid wire from Mrs Alf Davies to Charles Patterson of the Daily Recorder dispatched from Pendeen at 2.40 p.m. on Saturday, September 16:

Miss Weston and my husband visited Wheal Garth mine yesterday and have not returned stop Search party organized—Davies.

Transcript of a code wire from Detective-inspector Fuller to Superintendent McGlade at Scotland Yard dispatched from Pendeen at 2.50 p.m. on Saturday, September 16:

Maureen Weston and three local miners missing stop Went down Wheal Garth mine yesterday following visit previous day stop Am convinced she had discovered something stop Mine reportend to be unsafe stop Two falls heard late yesterday afternoon stop Locals fear they are trapped stop Rescue parties have opened up new shaft and are working desperately to clear falls stop Advise detention of Jesse Arthur Maclean late engineer to mine for questioning stop Description tall lean dark hair thinning glasses Scotch stop Also locate and detain Wilson—Fuller.

Record of a phone call put through by Superintendent McGlade of Scotland Yard to Chief-inspector Saviour of Durham at 3.45 p.m. on Saturday, September 16:

I want you to detain Jesse Arthur Maclean, engineer in charge of the mining work at the munitions dump at Dutton. You can do it under the Emergency Powers (Defence) Act—I've nothing against him so far.

Note from Superintendent McGlade to Colonel Blank at M.I.5 and dispatched by a special messenger at 5.30 p.m. on Saturday, September 16:

For your information I enclose copies of a number of letters and telegrams sent from a Miss Maureen Weston to Charles Patterson, news editor of the *Daily Recorder.* They may be of interest to you. You will remember she was investigating the disappearance of Walter Craig in the Cadgwith U-boat incident for her paper. I am detaining the man Maclean mentioned in her letters who is now working on a munitions dump and am endeavouring to discover the whereabouts of Tubby Wilson.

This file of communications received by Patterson from Miss Weston was handed to me this afternoon by Patterson himself after he had learned that the girl had not returned from an expedition into the Wheal Garth mine.

I should be glad to hear what you think of them.

Yours,
McGLADE.

Memorandum from the Naval Intelligence Department of the Admiralty to Colonel Blank of M.I.5 dispatched by special messenger at 8.45 p.m. on Saturday, September 16:

Here are details of reports of U-boats in the vicinity of the Cornish coast received since the outbreak of war from coastal patrols of the Navy and the Fleet Air Arm:

September 4, 51.12 north 51.48 west. September 6, 49.54 north 5.5 west. September 9, 49.51 north 3.36 west. September 10, 49.11 north 2.24 west. September 10, 51.8 north 5.21 west. September 13, 52.3 north 5.48 west. September 14, 50.17 north 5.54 west. September

15, 49.45 north 6.35 west. September 15, 50.25 north 5.31 west.

In most cases depth charges or bombs were released, but only in two cases has the destruction of the U-boat been definitely achieved. Hope this is what you wanted—F.E.

Communiques dispatched from the War Office and the Admiralty shortly after 9.30 p.m. on Saturday, September 16, as a result of phone calls from M.I.5:

From the War Office to officer commanding H.M. Forces encamped at Trereen, Cornwall:

Dispatch immediately two companies of infantry to Pendeen. One company is to mount guard on all exits of the Wheal Garth mine. If one company proves insufficient further troops must be dispatched. The second company is to enter the mine. Contact Detective-inspector Fuller of Scotland Yard who will be awaiting your arrival at the inn. He will provide guides to the mine and will inform you of the position.

From the Admiralty to commanders of destroyers EH 4 and EH 5 stationed at Newlyn:

Proceed immediately to 50 degrees 23 minutes north 5 degrees 43 minutes west and patrol West Cornish coast from Botallack Head to Pendeen Watch.

Part Three
The Wheal Garth Closes Down

1

Plans

With a sudden thrill of excitement I realized what Logan was doing. He was carrying on a conversation in morse. But was it a conversation? Was he making it up? I looked at what I had written down. It read: 'I came here with three miners. Progress into new workings blocked by falls. Had removed part of lightest fall and found way through when met by armed Germans. What is this place?'

I looked up at Logan. His face was intent on the movements of the spoon against the iron bars of the grille. Heavy tap, pause, four light taps, pause, tap tap, pause, tap tap tap, long pause, short short, pause, short short short, long pause, short short short, short short long—and so it went on. I did not understand morse, but I presumed he was replying to the question.

I looked down again at what I had written. It made sense. It suggested that this was part of a mine. That tied up with the idea of the base being either in Cornwall or in Spain. It certainly did not read like the imaginings of a man who was mentally sick. I got up and went over to the door. Logan had finished tapping. Faintly I heard a metallic click, then two more, louder and close together. Then short short short short, pause, dash dash dash. There was no doubt about it. Someone was morsing from the next cell. 'Who is it?' I asked Logan.

'That's just what he's asked us,' he replied. 'One of the first things he said when we established contact was that he represented the *Daily Recorder*. Evidently they sent someone out to

look for you.' He resumed his tapping with the spoon. I waited.
So Logan remembered his morse, did he?

He stopped tapping and listened. Then he took my pencil
and wrote down slowly in block letters—IS CRAIG REALLY
THERE. THIS IS MAUREEN WESTON. 'Good God, it's a
woman!' said Logan. Then he wrote: PATTERSON SENT ME
TO INVESTIGATE YOUR DISAPPEARANCE.

I was amazed. 'Ask her how she found us,' I said.

The spoon went tap-tap again and presently Logan began
writing the reply: 'Worked back from the spy at Carillon. This
led me to phoney mine owner. And this is the mine. It lies four
miles north of Saint Just.'

'So you were right,' I said. 'This base is in Cornwall. Ask her
whether any one knows where she is.'

Back came the reply: 'Please repeat slower. I am working the
code from a diary.'

Logan wielded the spoon again with longer pauses between
each letter. Then came the reply: 'Yes. But the Germans have
blown up galleries in old workings so that it will look as though
we have been trapped by a fall. Have you any plans?'

Heavy, light, pause, heavy heavy heavy went the tapping
of Logan's spoon. It was so short that I knew what that
must be. Then we were interrupted by the opening of the
guard-room door. Shortly afterwards our evening meal was
brought to us.

When we were alone again I said: 'You know, we've only got
till Sunday evening at the latest?'

He nodded with his mouth full of potato stew and contrived
to grin at the same time.

I looked at him closely. 'Do you remember who the owner
of Carillon was?' I asked.

'Ar, his name was Cutner—is that right?'

'Your memory is not so bad after all,' I said, 'I suppose it's all
come back to you?'

'That's right.' He nodded and grinned, and there was that twinkle in his eyes that I had not seen since Cadgwith.

I was still not altogether convinced. It seemed incredible that the man could have put an act over on me so completely. After all, I had been his constant companion for nearly two weeks. Anyway, I failed to see the necessity of it. I tried him with another question. 'Can you tell me the name of the coastguard at Cadgwith?' I asked, and there was a trace of anxiety in my voice, for I was desperately anxious for someone to share with me the responsibility of immobilizing the base.

'Let me see,' he hesitated, his Slav features puckered with amusement. 'It wouldn't be Ted Morgan, now, would it?'

I felt a sudden great relief. 'Thank God for that,' I breathed. 'But why the devil didn't you tell me you were only shamming?'

'I would have,' he said, 'but I figured it out that I'd have a better chance of putting it across if you thought I was going balmy too. Anyway, I'm no actor. I knew the only thing was to make myself believe I was balmy. I tell you, at times I was afraid I really was.'

I gave a short laugh. 'That's what most actors have discovered,' I said. 'But what was the idea?'

'I wanted to avoid giving them the information they were after. And also I thought it might help.'

'Well, it doesn't seem to have,' I said.

'Hasn't it?' He beckoned me across to his bed. 'Here's the result of my carving,' he said. He bent down and tilted the bed up so that he could get hold of the leg nearest the wall and farthest from the door. With the help of his knife he began to prise very carefully at one of the letters of his name which he had cut on the inside of the leg, low down. And in a second the whole section with his name had come away, and in a hollow cut below it was a key fitted snugly into the wood.

He put the section back and tapped it carefully into position.

It fitted perfectly and very tightly. Unless any one were looking for it, it was unlikely to be discovered. 'What key is it?' I asked.

'The key to this cell.'

'But how did you get hold of it?'

He returned to his stew. 'There are four cells along here,' he said, 'and the locks are all the same. Remember those ratings that were put in the other cells to cool off after a brawl last Monday? The guards used the same key for all the cells. And I noticed another thing. The guards were sometimes careless. They left the keys in the cell doors instead of returning them to the guard-room. So I started my craze for modelling and hollowed out my little hiding-place. Because I was supposed to be daft I got away with it. And two days after I had finished it I had the chance of lifting a key from the lock of the neighbouring cell. It was missed about two hours later. You remember we were searched on Wednesday night and the whole cell turned upside down by the guard? But by then it was safely tucked away.'

'I wonder they haven't put bolts on the door,' I said.

'Probably the guard didn't report the loss.'

I sat down on my bed again and considered the matter. It was certainly a step forward. We had the means of getting out of our cell at any time of the night. But having got out, what then? The various stores were all locked and we hadn't the key to any of these. That meant we could not get at either the fuel or the munitions. And the guards went the rounds every hour. Moreover, the arrival of Maureen Weston and her three miners complicated matters in that any plan to destroy the whole base meant the loss of their lives as well as ours.

The same thought seemed to have crossed Big Logan's mind, for he said: 'What's this Maureen Weston like?'

I cast my mind back to the time when she had been on the staff of the *Recorder*. 'She's small and dark and very attractive,' I said. 'She had Irish blood in her and as women go she's pretty tough.' I suddenly remembered that big men like small women. 'She's just your type if you're feeling repressed.'

He grinned. 'Sounds interesting,' he said. 'But just at the moment I was thinking out some way of destroying her and every one else in this base.'

'So was I,' I said. 'But how are we going to do it?'

'We should be able to deal with the guard. There are only two who actually do the rounds. All we have to do is to get the keys off them, go into the munitions store and blow the place up.'

'It sounds easy, put like that,' I said. 'But suppose we aren't able to deal with the guards silently and they rouse the base?'

'We'll have to take the chance. Even if they were able to give the alarm we'd still have plenty of time.'

'True,' I nodded, 'but, on the other hand, we can't afford to take chances. Can't we manage it without attacking the guards? What I've been thinking about is those six-inch guns on the submarines. You know how to handle them, don't you? The after gun on U 21 is in working order and the boat lies with its stern facing straight down the main cave. One shot with that would surely be sufficient to block the underwater entrance. That would stop the submarines leaving without destroying them.'

He shook his head. 'We must destroy the submarines,' he said. 'They might blast their way out through the cliff. And the only way to destroy the boats is to blow the place up. Your scheme would only work if we could get out of the place ourselves and warn the naval authorities.'

'Listen!' I said. The relief of being able to discuss the position with someone instead of just lying and racking my brains had made me somewhat excited. 'Maureen has brought three miners with her. If we could release them and, after firing the gun, get into the landward exit with picks and so on, we might be able to get through the falls they have made this afternoon.'

At that he laughed. 'Do you know what a bad fall of rock in a Cornish tin mine is like?' he demanded. 'There's maybe a hundred feet of roof brought down along our exit gallery. And the blockage will be caused by huge chunks of granite. And you suggest three miners get through it with picks!'

'Well, there are mobile drills in the base,' I said, a trifle put out.

At that he stopped grinning and said: 'So there are.' He sat silent for a moment, stroking his beard. 'The trouble is they'd guess where we had gone. As soon as they had searched the base, they'd be after us, and we shouldn't have a dog's chance.'

'I'm not so sure,' I said. 'In the first place they would probably be too worried about other things to come after us for some time, and by then we could have partially blocked the exit gallery behind us. For another, we could lay for the guards and if successful, arm ourselves at the expense of the base. What I mean is that, though I think it rather risky to be dependent upon a successful attack on the guards for our means of destroying the base, I think we might deal with the guards as well as man the gun. If we succeeded with the guards we should have about ten minutes, maybe quarter of an hour, in which to ransack the base for the equipment and weapons we required. If we didn't succeed, then we'd be no worse off. With the gun loaded and sighted, it would only be a matter of an instant to fire.'

Logan snapped his fingers. 'Sure and I believe you've got it,' he said. 'The next thing to do is to get in touch with this Weston girl again and find out what part of the base she came out into.'

At that moment we were interrupted by the arrival of the guard to collect our empty stew cans. 'You'd better get some sleep,' he said in German, pointing to our beds and laying his hands against his cheek to indicate what he meant. 'Two submarines are coming in tonight.' He held up two fingers in front of my face and said: 'Boats.'

I thanked him and he departed smiling. He was one of the

nicest of our guards, a large fellow with a frank open face and a ridiculous little moustache. I passed the information on to Logan. 'Thank God, they're both coming in tonight,' I said. 'That leaves tomorrow night free. Unless of course U 47 doesn't leave tonight, as planned.'

He got up and went over to the door. In his hand he held the knife he had used to hollow out the leg of his bed. But there seemed much more activity than usual in the gallery. In fact, it was not until nearly ten o'clock that he was able to establish contact with Maureen Weston. Movement in the gallery outside remained remarkably active, and as a result he was not able to keep up a sustained conversation. What he learned was very damping to our spirits. The mine gallery by which she and her companions had reached the base entered it by way of a recess in the guard-room. Moreover, the mine gallery was practically blocked about two hundred feet from the base.

This meant that the possibility of getting anything like a mobile drill through was small and in any case the chances of ever having the opportunity of entering the mine by way of the guard-room seemed somewhat remote. I understood now the cause of the activity in the gallery outside and the continual movement of men in and out of the guard-room opposite. It was from the guard-room that they were prepared to meet an attack. Probably they had machine-guns ready mounted in the mine galleries in case miners cleared the falls.

But this activity did not explain the faint but persistent clatter of electric welders and the muffled roar of machinery. Usually at this time of night the base was comparatively quiet, save for the hum of the dynamos and the murmur of voices. But for the fact that my watch said it was ten-twenty I should have said it was day-time. It could mean only one thing. 'They're rushing the repairs to U 21,' I said.

Logan nodded. 'I'm afraid they are,' he agreed. 'Which means that they're going to send the boats out tomorrow night and not Sunday.'

'Maybe they'll get some away tonight.'

'Hell! I wish I hadn't left it so late.'

'Why did you?' I asked. 'For the same reason that I did?'

'What was that?'

'Oh, just that I put it off until I couldn't put it off any longer.'

'Perhaps,' he said. 'Also I wanted to get the maximum number of boats in the base. Your friend Maureen doesn't seem to have helped us much.'

'Except in so far as her disappearance may make people suspicious about this mine. Patterson is no fool.'

'But why should they suspect that there is something wrong with the mine? The girl goes down with three miners to look over it and doesn't appear again. Two deep rumbling sounds are heard—an explosion or a fall? A search party is organized. They find the workings blocked by a big fall. Every one is then satisfied as to the reason why she and her companions never got back.'

'That depends on Patterson,' I said. 'Ask her how often she was reporting to Patterson and how much she has told him about the mine.'

But to get a message through now took some time owing to the activity outside. In all I think it was nearly half an hour before we got the full reply. It came through bit by bit as opportunity offered. It read: 'Patterson has no idea mine is submarine base. All he knows is that I was suspicious of it and that on the first occasion I went down I found falls that should not have been there and that looked unnatural.'

'And that's that,' said Logan, returning to his bed.

'Patterson is no fool,' I reiterated. 'And he's got the sharpest nose for news of any man I know. I think he'll move heaven and earth to get the mine opened up.'

'Ar, that may be so, but who is going to do the opening up?

To clear a big fall of rock takes time and costs a deal of money. Who is going to pay for it—not the paper, I know.'

'Well, it's our only hope,' I said, 'if they send the boats out tomorrow night.'

At that moment the key grated in the lock and one of the guards came in. The first of the two U-boats was coming in and we were marched down to the docks.

We had a wait of more than fifteen minutes in the cold damp atmosphere of No. 3 dock with the constant chugging of the donkey engine echoing from the main cave. In the course of this time I gained several pieces of interesting information. All work had been suspended on U 47 and she would not be ready to go out until Sunday night at the earliest. The whole engineering effort of the base was being concentrated on U 21 and the word had apparently gone out that she must be ready for active service by tomorrow afternoon—that was Saturday. This confirmed my belief that the whole fleet would go out on the Saturday and not the Sunday night. There was a rumour that the boat coming in now was the one that had sunk the *Athenia*. And there was also talk that the second boat was already waiting to come in. That meant that in a few hours' time there would be no less than six of Germany's largest ocean-going U-boats in the base, as well as the store barge.

I passed on the information to Logan. But I did not hear his comment for there was a sudden swirl of water in the dock and a large wave slid quietly along it, overflowing on to the dockside and thoroughly wetting our feet. There was much seething of water in the main cave, then the slam of metal against metal, followed by prolonged cheers. The first of the two U-boats had arrived.

The diminutive diesel-engined tug fussed noisily about the main cave and in a few minutes the bows of the U-boat appeared opposite No. 3 dock. A rope was tossed on to the dockside and we passed it from hand to hand. As soon as it was fully manned the order was given to heave and we dug our heels into the uneven rock floor and strained at the rope. Slowly the boat slid into the dock, the ratings that lined her decks fending her off from the sides with boat-hooks.

You seldom realize how wide a submarine is below the surface until you see one manoeuvred into a confined space. Empty, the dock presented quite a wide surface of water, oily and glinting in the electric light. But the U-boat filled it from side to side, and her conning tower almost touched the roof of the cave. I could not help feeling then how entirely insulated this base was from the outside world. It was, in fact, a world of its own. And after a fortnight there it seemed to me quite possible that no other world existed, that my memories of green fields, of huddles of white cottages among the Cornish cliffs, of Piccadilly, of factories and ships were all a dream, and that this was the only reality. And now here was this U-boat come from that other world with probably Kiel as its last port of call.

As soon as the boat had been made fast the crew were assembled and marched off to their quarters. Normally we should have then been taken back to our cells. But on this occasion we were taken to the next dock, No. 4, where the U 21 lay. Men were required to assist in moving the for'ard six-inch gun from the electric trolley on which it had been taken to the foundry, back on to the deck of the submarine. Repairs to the gun had been completed.

There was ten minutes' back-breaking work as it was lifted on pulleys attached to the steel derrick and swung, largely by brute force, into position. It was while this was happening that a slight accident occurred which had a wholly disproportionate influence on what happened later. The commander of U 21 had come down to welcome the Number One of the boat that had just come in, U 27, who was apparently a particular friend. And having seen him to his quarters, he came down to see how the engineers were getting on with his own boat. He was smoking a cigarette. This was strictly against regulations, but no one seemed inclined to point that out to him. There came a moment in the hoisting of the gun when every man was required to strain his utmost to keep the mountings from swinging against the side of the submarine. The commander did not hesitate, but threw his weight in with the rest. It reminded me of a scrum down. We were all pushing against each other with our heads down until at last the mounting was clear of the deck and was allowed to swing slowly inwards.

We were just straightening our aching backs and getting our breath back when suddenly somebody said: 'There's something burning.' The acrid smell of smouldering rags seemed all around us. Then something flared up by one of the legs of the derrick. For a split second every one stood motionless and my mind recorded a vivid impression as though I were looking at a still from a film. Then one of the engineers dived at the flames and began stamping them out with his feet. What had happened was that the commander had thrown the stub of his cigarette away before helping with the gun, and it had set fire to a mass of oil-sodden rags. Probably they were impregnated with petrol as well. Before the engineer could muffle them the flames had caught at his overalls and the oil in them was burning.

The U-boat commander ripped off his jacket and flung it round the man's burning legs. For a second every one seemed to forget about the fire itself, which was now flaring noisily and causing some to move back on account of the heat of it. Moreover, the dockside itself, impregnated with oil, was alight in places. Having settled the engineer's trousers, the commander flung his jacket on to the flames and stamped them under with his feet.

By this time we were all coughing with the smoke, which was very heavy now that the flames themselves were muffled. As he stamped with his feet the commander kept coughing. I could see the sweat gathering in beads on his forehead. Then suddenly his knees seemed to sag under him and he collapsed.

One man pulled him clear of the smouldering pile of rags, while two others finished the job of extinguishing the fire.

The doctor was sent for, but it was some time before the commander came round and every one who had been standing near the fire seemed to be feeling queer. One man actually fainted, but recovered as soon as he had been laid out a little farther down the dock. I myself found difficulty in breathing and my head reeled as though I were a little drunk. Logan, too, complained of feeling peculiar.

Then the order was given to get over to No. 1 dock as the second submarine was coming in. It was shouted by the officer in charge of the fatigue from the end of the dock. Some men obeyed, but the majority were too busy getting their breath back or arguing as to the cause of the trouble. The order was repeated. But instead of obeying it Logan swung himself on to U 21 and joined the engineers in their struggle to lower the gun into its correct position. I followed him. We had lost touch with our guards. The gun was eased into its mountings. The operation took about three minutes and gave us ample opportunity to look around. But the result was most discouraging. Even ready-use ammunition was stowed below deck and it was quite impossible to get at the armoured ammunition truck.

Our guard then re-established contact with us. As we climbed down on to the dockside I saw that the commander was now on his feet again, looking very white and his clothes in a filthy state. He still seemed a bit short of breath. The doctor said something about asphyxiation, but I couldn't hear the whole sentence. We were marched down to No. 1 dock. The fatigue party had already manned the hawser and I could see the dark pointed bows of the submarine nosing into the dock. As we took our place, Logan said: 'What was the matter with him?'

'Asphyxiation of some sort,' I said.

'Yes, but why did we all suffer from it? What caused it?'

I said I didn't know, but presumed it was something to do

with the burning waste. Our conversation was interrupted by the order to heave. As soon as the submarine had been made fast, the fatigue party was dismissed and we were taken back to our cell.

When the door was closed Logan said: 'This is a helluva mess. Your idea of manning the after gun of U 21 is quite hopeless.'

'You mean we can't get hold of the ammunition?' I said.

'Not only that. There's the guard. It wasn't until I saw the one on the bridge that I remembered they mount two guards on every submarine in the base day and night. The other was in the bows.'

I nodded. I was feeling very despondent. When I had discovered that Logan was as alive as I was to the situation, I had for some reason felt that success was assured. His great bulk gave one confidence where it was a question of action.

Not only were the guns out of the question, but we had only twenty-four hours in which to carry out any plan. And throughout that time the base would be a hive of activity. It was, as Logan put it—a hell of a mess. Failure would mean the loss of hundreds of British lives. Moreover, it would mean a severe blow to British prestige, and might as a result seriously affect the course of the war, for neutral opinion was a vital factor in the initial stages. I had a sudden picture of those four great ships of the Atlantic squadron wallowing up the Channel, of periscopes cutting the water inside the screening destroyers, of sudden explosions and the sterns of those proud ships lifting as they sank. It was not to be thought of. Something had to be done.

'Well?' Logan said.

I began removing my wet shoes and socks. 'Looks as though we make a desperate attack on the guard,' I said.

'When?' he asked. 'Tonight?' His tone was sarcastic. He had taken off his dungarees and was climbing into bed. 'I'm going to sleep on it,' he announced.

'But, good God, man,' I said, 'this is the last full night we've got in which to do something.'

'And the base full of men repairing things. Did you see No. 3 dock after we had berthed that last submarine? The stores department were already at work replenishing the supplies. They'll be at it all night—food, water, munitions. U 21 has got to be finished by tomorrow afternoon. You told me so yourself. And every other boat in the base will have to be ready for sea by then. We'll have to wait. If we left this cell now every one we met would wonder what we were up to. But if we left it in the day-time—say, when we were having tea—no one would pay any attention to us. They'd just think we were on fatigue. They're used to seeing us around the base in the day-time.'

'I see your point,' I said, and put the light out and climbed into bed. He was right, of course, but at the same time it made it a rather last-minute job. The truth was that now zero-hour had been definitely fixed my whole soul revolted against it. It is extraordinary how powerful the will to live is in the average human being. If it had been a question of immediate action, I could have faced it. Subconsciously, I suppose, I had keyed myself to expect action that night. I had felt that it was tonight or never as soon as I knew for certain that the boats were going out the following night. And I honestly believe that if it had been a question of instantaneous action, I would have walked out of that cell and blown the whole place up quite calmly. But to plan such an action sixteen hours in advance somehow revolted me.

Sleep was out of the question. I simply lay in the darkness and thought and thought till plans went round in my head without meaning. And as I became more and more mentally tired, my plans gained in phantasy until they had no relation to reality whatsoever. Schemes for blasting a way out through the cliff by firing a six-inch gun like a machine-gun, for escaping through the main entrance in diving suits, for constructing all sorts of Heath Robinson contrivances to blow the base up without killing myself rattled round my brain. I even remembered the strata of limestone I had discovered and thought of drilling through that to the main shaft of the mine or burning piles of oil-impregnated cotton waste in order to asphyxiate Fulke.

And then for some reason I was awake. It did not take me long to discover the reason. My subconscious schemes were still clear in my head and I realized that my mind had connected the limestone strata and the burning waste and I was back in my schooldays listening to a rather portly man with a mortarboard and horn-rimmed spectacles initiating myself and about fifteen others into the mysteries of chemistry.

I leant over and shook Big Logan. Instantly it seemed he was wide awake. I heard him sit up in his bed. 'What is it?' he asked.

'Listen!' I said. I was excited. 'Do you know what happens to limestone when it's heated? It gives off carbon dioxide and leaves calcium oxide, which is quick lime. If I remember rightly the equation is—$CaCo_3 = CaO + CO_2$.'

'How does that help?' he asked.

'Well, don't you see? Carbon dioxide is poisonous when it replaces air—lack of oxygen causes suffocation. That's what happened to the commander of U 21 tonight. There's a strata of limestone running down No. 4 dock and across into the storage cave opposite, and it broadens out to a width of about five feet at the entrance to the store. That burning waste was lying on this strata of limestone and was giving off CO_2. The commander passed out through lack of oxygen and we were all affected slightly. Now, suppose we could get a really big fire going on the limestone.'

'And then ask the commander of the base to hold a scouts' jamboree round it,' suggested Logan.

'I'm serious,' I said.

'I know you are,' he said. 'You've been lying awake thinking up all sorts of impossible schemes to avoid being killed yourself.'

It was a direct accusation of cowardice and I resented it, largely because I knew it to be true. 'I was only trying to think out a scheme that had a chance,' I said. 'I'm not afraid of dying.'

'Well, I am, if it's unnecessary,' he replied.

'Then think up something better,' I said, and turned over.

He did not reply, and when I had recovered from my resentment at his attitude, I began to consider the scheme in detail. Certainly the bald outline I had given did not sound particularly convincing. Several questions immediately leapt to my mind. First, how were we to make the necessary fire without it being put out before it had got to work on the limestone? Second, how were we to immunize ourselves? Third, what about Maureen and her companions? And fourth, was the ventilation system so good that it would be impossible to get sufficient CO_2 into the base to render every one unconscious?

I began to consider these questions one by one. The first, of course, depended upon circumstances. It was a matter for action when the opportunity offered. Tanks of oil and petrol were often being trundled round the base when a submarine was being refuelled. I had a box of matches in the pocket of my dungarees. A drum would have to be broached and some of its contents poured over the limestone strata. The flames would then have to be fed. A mixture of oil and petrol would be best. Then we should want picks and shovels to break up the limestone and build it round the flames. Moreover, the flames must not be allowed to spread—there was a good deal of oil on the docksides and in the dock gallery. What we really ought to do was to build a little circle of broken limestone and pour petrol and oil into the centre. Then there was the question of our own immunization. I began to see the reason for Logan's sarcasm.

At that moment Logan turned over towards me and said: 'What exactly is the effect of carbon dioxide? Does it kill a person?'

'It's not exactly poisonous, like coal gas,' I said. 'It just uses up the oxygen in the atmosphere. You saw the effects this evening. A man gets dizzy and then passes out. Put him in the fresh air and he comes round again. But I believe it can be lethal if it goes on long enough.'

Then he began asking all the questions that I had been asking myself. And the more we discussed it the more elaborate and impossible the whole thing seemed. To immunize ourselves we needed an oxygen cylinder. How were we to get hold of one? True, there were plenty in the base, but would one be around just when we wanted it? Then there was the question of the four other prisoners. Logan said: 'They would have to take their chance. In a locked cell they might not come off too badly and you say we can revive them with oxygen.' As to the air conditioning, Logan pointed out that fresh air was brought in through a hole drilled in the cliff above the underwater entrance and the stale air was driven out through the look-out hole, the entrance to which led off the upper galleries. 'That means the carbon dioxide would circulate through the entire base,' he said.

But though this seemed to help, I must admit I had by then come to the conclusion that the scheme was unworkable. And after we had talked it over for some time, I said: 'For heaven's sake try to think out some scheme by which we can get at the munitions store and blow the place up.' I was by then tired and discouraged. We discussed various plans for dealing with our guards at a time when the munitions store was open, getting into it and using one of the many mines stored there to explode the place. But Logan kept reverting to my own scheme and asking questions. I suppose my brain must have been tired out, for my answers became more and more vague, and the next thing I remember is being shaken by the guard and told to get up. I looked at my watch. It was seven o'clock and my breakfast of porridge, bread and jam and tea was lying on the floor beside me.

2

Action

Logan was already seated on his bed, eating his porridge. As the door closed behind the guard, I said: 'Well, have you decided on any plan of action?'

He shook his head and continued eating. 'We'll have to take advantage of any opportunities that offer,' he said. He made no mention of my own scheme, and frankly, when I came to consider it with the prospect of putting it into action within the next few hours, it did not seem practicable. There were so many snags. I felt nervous and depressed. We had no plan, and yet we had to do something within the next twelve hours.

When he had finished his porridge, Logan knelt down on the floor and removed the key from its hiding-place. 'What do you want that for?' I asked, as he slipped it inside one of his socks and began putting on his shoes, which were still wet from the previous night.

'We may need it,' he said.

Even then, though I knew he had no plan, he gave me confidence. It wasn't just a question of his strength. There was something solid about the man, and I thanked God that his brain was all right and that I had not got to carry out some desperate plan on my own. At that moment I wished that my experience on the *Daily Recorder* had been as a reporter and not as dramatic critic. I could think of one or two men in the news-room who would have revelled in a situation like this, men who had lived on their wits and knocked about the world all their lives. I had never had to use my wits as a means of livelihood in that sense.

How much Big Logan had had to use his wits, as opposed to brute force, I did not know, but his swift adaptation to circumstances on the cliffs above the Devil's Frying Pan and later in the U-boat was encouraging.

Almost before we had finished breakfast, the guard was back again. But instead of beginning the morning's work in the latrines and kitchens, we were taken straight down to the docks and set to work carrying stores from the store-rooms to U 54, which was the boat that had come into No. 1 dock the previous night. This seemed promising, for No. 1 dock was the nearest to the munitions store. And I felt a distinct zero-hour feeling within me.

We obtained the stores from No. 1 store-room, directly opposite the dock. That meant crossing the main gallery and entering an electrically-lit tunnel, protected by sheet metal doors, that led to the store itself. These doors now stood open and the key was in the lock. It would take only a matter of a second to close the doors and lock them. That would look after the provisioning officer of U 54 and the four men who were working under him in the store. The trouble was that, though our own two guards did not present much difficulty since they had become accustomed to us and regarded us as quite harmless—it must be remembered that Logan was still a mental defective to all who knew him in the base—there were the customary two guards on the U-boat itself, one standing on the bridge and the other near the bows, as well as several men lifting the stores from the deck, where we placed them, and passing them into the submarine through an after-hatch. Even supposing we were able to deal with all these, there was still the problem of the guards to the munitions store. I had never been into this store. Only certain men were allowed in. But I had been as far as the entrance. A huge steel bulkhead had been built across the entrance in an effort to protect the base from any mishap. The door through this bulkhead was only just wide enough to take a munitions trolley. The guards were stationed one on either side of the tunnel that led off the main dock gallery just beyond No. 1 dock.

The prospect seemed hopeless. But at least we were near the munitions dump, and I was keyed up ready for a desperate attempt. But Logan made no move, even when we were joined by three more men, dressed in dungarees like ourselves. They were under a guard of two ratings and a petty officer, and were presumably Maureen Weston's miners. The guard complicated the position, for, unlike our own guards, they were watchful of the new-comers. But the miners did represent an addition to our force, especially as they looked to me about the toughest trio I had ever set eyes on. One, who seemed to be their leader, was short and bow-legged, and had a Welsh accent. The other two were undoubtedly Cornish. Whether Logan thought that their usefulness was cancelled out by the guard they had brought, I do not know, but when I asked him in a whisper if he was going to make a move, he replied: 'Not yet.'

Once we had to go to the foundry, which was right at the other end of the dock gallery, to collect the conning tower hatch, which had been fitted with a new rubber jointing ring. The activity along the whole gallery and in most of the docks was terrific, especially in docks 3 and 4. When we passed No. 4, fresh water was being run into U 21 from a mobile tank and torpedoes were being hoisted aboard from a munitions truck. Riveting had ceased, but engineers were still at work on one of the A.A. guns. The boat that had come into No. 3 dock the night before was being provisioned and fuelled.

Listening to the talk of the men, I found there were only two topics of conversation—the coming action and the rumour of a woman in the base. No statement had been issued about the previous day's alarm, but it seemed to be generally known that certain prisoners had arrived in the base, including a woman. Doubtless the emergency guards had passed on the information to their friends. What interested me was the effect that the unseen presence of a woman in this monastic place had on different men. Those who had been stationed on the Atlantic trade routes and at the base long before war broke out had not seen a woman now for some months. Some became sentimental and talked of their sweethearts and wives. But the majority seemed to take it as a great joke and already obscene stories, based on Maureen's presence in the base, were going the rounds. It seemed strange that I should see this stock theatrical situation actually happening in real life, especially against such a novel background.

But though a girl's presence in the base was something of a sensation, the coming action was the main topic of conversation. I realized then how similar must be the feelings of these men to my own at that moment. Zero-hour for them was somewhere about midnight. At present they were safe enough, if somewhat bored. But tonight they were leaving the safety of the base for the unknown. The chances of ever returning were not great, they knew that. And like me, probably their best chance of remaining alive rested in failure.

About eleven o'clock, when we had completed the piling of the necessary stores on the after deck of U 54, Logan and I were marched off to our usual job of emptying the latrines. Death has its compensations! When we had finished we were marched back to the docks, and joined the three new prisoners at carrying stores to U 21. The dockside seemed littered with stores of various kinds. There were cases of margarine and jam, tins of biscuits, cardboard cases full of tinned foods and packets of coffee, sugar, salt, and all sorts of other foodstuffs. The three miners had carried all this from No. 4 store and were piling it on the dockside, opposite the after-hatch. Mines were being loaded into the after-minelaying compartments and a huge tank of oil had been brought on to the dock on a trolley. There was also a smaller tank of petrol. But refuelling operations had not yet begun.

We stood about for a time, and then several of the crew,

together with the cook, arrived. The after-hatch was opened and they descended into the bowels of the submarine. We then brought a small gangway and laid it from the dockside to the submarine. Our job was to carry the stores from the dock to the submarine and lower them through the after-hatch on a rope.

It was now nearly twelve—first lunch. There were two lunch times—twelve and twelve-thirty. This made it easier for the kitchen staff when there were a large number in the base, as there were now, and at the same time enabled any rush work to be carried on without any complete stoppage for the midday meal.

We had not been carrying on this work long when, just as I was lowering a case of margarine down the hatch, I saw Logan time his arrival at a pile of cases at the same moment as the little leader of the miners arrived with the next load. I could not be sure, but I felt convinced that Logan said something to the man. I did not get an opportunity to speak to Logan for some time, but I noticed that the miners, instead of putting the cases down anyhow, were piling them on top of one another, so that they made a sort of wall of cases across the dockside.

Convinced that something was afoot, I gradually speeded up my work so that, instead of alternating with Logan, I was bringing my cases up just behind him. At last I managed it so that I put my case down on the deck of the submarine at the same time as he put his down. I had just opened my mouth to question him when he whispered: 'Stand by.'

A few minutes later orders were suddenly shouted from the main gallery. I glanced at my watch. It was midday. I looked down the length of the submarine. Men in their white uniforms were passing along the gallery in the direction of the ramp leading to the upper galleries. The docks were much quieter now and there was far less movement of men up and down the gallery at the end of the dock.

I took a quick look round at the disposition of the guards as I walked off the submarine. Our own two guards were standing chatting beside the pile of cases. One was actually leaning on them. The U-boat guard was now reduced to one and he was standing on the deck for'ard of the conning tower. The other guard was on duty inside the submarine as base personnel were now storing munitions. A munitions trolley loaded with shells was standing on the dockside. Another gangway had been thrown from the dockside to the deck of the submarine and these shells were being carried in through the for'ard hatch. At the moment the trolley, with upwards of twenty shells on it, was standing deserted on the dockside, the personnel having gone to first lunch. There remained only the miners' guard of a petty officer and two ratings.

I was now following close behind Logan and feeling uncom-fortably self-conscious. Our guards were deep in conversation, with their backs half-turned to us. As we approached the pile of cases, one of them looked round. I could not believe he would not notice the air of expectation about me. We each took hold of a case of canned goods. The guard turned to answer a question the other had put. Logan carefully replaced his case. Then he straightened up. Until then I don't think I had realized how enormous his hands were. He stretched them out and took each of the guards by the throat. His body seemed to brace itself and the muscles of his arms swelled as he forced those two men silently to the ground behind the barrier of packing cases. They seemed to lose consciousness without even a kick.

'Get into his uniform,' he said, pointing to the smaller of the two men.

I did not hesitate. The die was cast now. We could not go back. And strangely enough, now that I had something to do, I did not feel in the least nervous.

Logan glanced over the boxes and then picked up a case and took it on to the deck of the submarine. Feverishly I worked

171

at the uniform of the guard, afraid that at any moment he might become conscious again or that the miners' guard would reappear. By the time Logan was back I had got the uniform off the man. One by one he banged their heads sharply against the rock floor. I thought he had smashed their skulls, but he must have seen my look of horror, for he said: 'It's all right. Only making certain that they stay out.'

It was a matter of seconds for me to slip into the man's uniform. Logan glanced once more round the store boxes. Then he dragged the man whose uniform I had borrowed to one side and covered him with cases. Then he said: 'Step out on to the deck and call to the petty officer of the guard. His name is Kammel. Just call his name and beckon to him.'

I did as he told me. I stepped out from behind the cases. 'Herr Kammel!' I called. 'Here!' And I nodded to him with my head. He came at once and I stepped back behind the cases. Logan told me to kneel down and pretend to be examining the unconscious guard. I knelt down and supported the man's head with my arm.

The footsteps of the petty officer rang sharply on the rock as he approached. I never saw the blow, but I heard it. It was a low dull thud and was accompanied by the sound of splintering bone. I felt slightly sick as I looked up and saw Big Logan holding the man by the scruff of his neck like a puppy as he lowered his unconscious body beside the other. The man's mouth was hanging open. The jaw had obviously been broken.

There remained the two ratings. And then there was the guard still standing serenely on the deck of the submarine just in front of the conning tower. Looking over the cases, I could just see part of his uniform and his right hand. The three miners had just appeared out of the store at the end of the dock and were being escorted towards us by their guard. 'What do we do now?' I asked Logan.

'Get the guard,' he said, and bending down he removed the

petty officer's revolver from its holster. 'When they come up to the cases, you be bending down over the petty officer and tell them to get hold of his legs and shoulders. Make your voice sound as though it were urgent. I'll do the rest.' He pushed the unconscious guard, who had acted as decoy for the petty officer, under the cases with his mate, and then waited, the revolver behind his back.

I bent down and lifted the petty officer's head. I waited until I heard the sound of cases being stacked and then I called out in German to the two ratings. 'The petty officer has fainted,' I said. 'Come and help me lift him.' I heard their boots on the rock behind me. I did not dare look up. It was a nasty moment. I was dressed as a rating and consequently could not give them an order.

'What's the matter with him?' asked one. He spoke with a soft Bavarian accent.

'I don't know,' I said. 'You take his feet.'

Out of the tail of my eye I saw him take hold of the petty officer's feet. But the other man remained standing, obviously expecting me to take hold of the arms. 'You take his arms,' I said, and began to unbutton the petty officer's tunic and loosen his collar.

There was a moment's hesitation, and then the man bent down and slipped his hands beneath the officer's armpits. I remember noticing that his nails were unpleasantly bitten. 'Ready?' I said. And at the same moment came the sickening thud of metal on bone. As the man holding the petty officer's feet collapsed, I straightened up and covered the other with my revolver. He was too surprised to cry out. He looked from the fallen man to me with his mouth agape, and in that second strong hands gripped him by the throat. I looked round as the man slid unconscious to the floor. The little bow-legged miner was standing over him. I got to my feet. It had all happened in a flash. When I looked over the barricade of cases, I could see

173

no one on the dockside. The guard on the U-boat was still standing just for'ard of the conning tower.

'Get into these uniforms as quick as you can,' Logan told the three miners. 'And if any of them come round, you know what to do.' Then he nodded to me and lifted one of the cases. I followed him up the gangway, my revolver swinging from its lanyard. He lowered the case through the hatch. Then we moved quickly for'ard, the grey curved bulk of the conning tower between us and the last remaining guard.

We stopped at the after gun. 'Get him round here,' Logan whispered. 'Pretend you've discovered something wrong with the gun. Keep your face turned away from the light.'

I nodded. '*Wache!*' I called. Then I repeated it. '*Wache!*' There was the sound of boots on hollow steel and the ring of a rifle butt. Unlike our own guards, who were armed with revolvers, the ratings that provided the U-boat guards were equipped with rifles and had bayonets fixed. I pointed to the telescopic sights at the side of the gun. 'Someone seems to have broken this,' I said.

It was simple. He peered at the sight. The next second I had caught hold of him as he fell. He never made a sound as Logan hit him. We laid him out on the deck. 'Quick!' said Logan. He ran to the ladder leading to the bridge. I followed him. At the top he paused. Someone was passing along the gallery at the end of the dock. I glanced back. Our miners were now struggling into the uniforms. I looked up at Logan. He seemed very different from the friendly Cornish fisherman I had known—and very different indeed from the friendly half-wit the base had known. His face had an intent purposeful look and that huge bulk that had been a harmless spectacle to the German ratings now seemed most sinister. It seemed to me scarcely credible that the man should have dealt so silently and so swiftly with no less than four armed guards.

Logan waited until the man had passed the end of the gallery and then, in a flash, he was on the bridge, had tumbled down the conning tower hatch. I followed him. We passed the control room and moved silently forward. Both of us had our revolvers ready. Then Logan hesitated and nodded to me to go forward. We had reached a bulkhead. Beyond it I could see our last guard. He was leaning against a rack of rifles, humming to himself. I went in, my hand on my revolver. At the sound of my footsteps, he sprang to attention, thinking I was an officer. The butt of his rifle rang on the steel floor plates. 'Give me that rifle,' I said in German. And I stepped forward and grabbed hold of it. His first instinct was to obey the order, and before he had realized that Big Logan was covering him with a revolver, the weapon was in my hands.

'March him aft,' Logan said.

I gave the order and we went clattering down the gangway past the control room and the ward-room and into the storage chamber. Here three men and an officer were busy dealing with the cases that we had lowered through the hatch. They turned as we entered. They were unarmed and could do nothing.

'Tell them that I'll shoot the first man that utters a sound,' Logan said.

I told them.

'Now get up through that hatch and have all our late guards dropped down here,' Logan said to me.

I ran up that little ladder and out on to the deck again. As soon as I had signalled to the three men on the dockside to bring the bodies on board I ran for'ard and got hold of the guard we had knocked out by the after gun. When we had lowered the bodies we closed the hatch. Almost immediately the men inside were attempting to force it open. I sent two of the miners to bring the heaviest articles they could find on the dockside with which to pin it down. The largest of them, whose uniform incidentally was much too small for him, stood with me on the hatch and held it down. In a few seconds the other two returned, struggling with a small portable forge, which is part of the equipment of every submarine. It had been left against the wall of the dock and weighed several hundredweight. It was a most effective weight and we placed it on the hatch. Then the miner I had detailed to mount guard went for'ard.

By this time I was beginning to get anxious about Logan, who had not yet reappeared. I felt at any moment men might come on to the dock. Moreover, there was the possibility that the men in the store-room at the end of the dock might get curious as to why the prisoners were no longer collecting the cases. I hurried for'ard to the conning tower. As I climbed the ladder to the bridge, Logan's head appeared in the hatch. He carried a light machine-gun and several magazines. 'Get that trolley alongside the gun,' he said.

'Are they the right shells?' I asked.

'I don't know,' was his reply. 'We'll have to see.'

I signalled to the men aft and jumped on to the dockside. I walked down to where the munitions trolley stood. The little bow-legged miner seemed intelligent, for he appeared to understand what I was up to, and he and his companion, the big man who had helped me hold the hatch down, brought the gangway along. The iron wheels of the trolley clattered noisily as I dragged it along the dock.

Suddenly there was a shout from behind me and I spun round, my hand moving automatically to my revolver. A man was standing in the doorway of the store-room. 'What have you done with those damned prisoners?' he shouted. Someone passing along the gallery stopped to see what the trouble was.

I thought we were for it. 'The lieutenant wants them to clear this pile of cases off the dock before they bring any more,' I shouted back to him in German. 'And he wants these shells got off the dock.'

The man hesitated, and then shrugged his shoulders. 'Well, hurry up,' he grumbled. 'It's nearly lunch-time.' He went back into the store-room and the man who had paused in the gallery continued on his way. I thanked God for my knowledge of German and dragged the trolley level with the gun.

By this time the two miners had placed the gangway in position and we each took a shell up on to the deck of the submarine. Big Logan was already bending over the gun. As I climbed up on the deck, I saw the muzzle of it slowly falling as Logan sighted it on the far end of the main cave. As I reached him he flung the breech open. I slipped the shell in. It fitted perfectly. He closed the breech and straightened his back. 'There we are,' he said. 'Everything ship-shape and ready to fire. All you have to do now is pull that lanyard.' He pointed to the trigger lanyard. 'Then you fling open the breech—so. The used shell falls out, in with the next and fire.'

The two miners put their shells down beneath the gun.

'Do you know how to fire a machine-gun?' Logan asked them.

'We were both in the last war,' replied the little bow-legged one, whom I later discovered to be Alf Davies, one-time foreman at the Wheal Garth.

'All right.' Logan turned to me. 'Will you take charge?' he said. 'There are rifles, hand-grenades and any other weapons you fancy in the submarine where we found that guard. Get what you want. Fire the gun only when there is no chance of holding the dock any longer. But it must be fired. I'm going to collect that girl.'

I said: 'Don't be a fool, Logan. You haven't a hope.'

'I've got the key,' he said. 'I'm still daft, remember. I think I'll get away with it.'

'Anyway, what's the good of bringing her down here?' I demanded. 'It's certain death.'

'That's where you're wrong,' he said. 'There's just a chance. I found three engineers in the engine-room and I've shut them in. All we've got to do is flood the dock and float the submarine out stern first. The tide is only about an hour on the turn. If we hurry we'll just be able to do it. Once out in the main cave we submerge and get out through the undersea entrance under our own power.'

'Good God, what a chance!' I exclaimed, thinking of the masses of complicated machinery with which the boat was filled. 'There isn't a hope.'

'Maybe not, but can you suggest anything else?' he asked. 'The mine is blocked, remember.'

I couldn't, and he jumped on to the dockside. I watched him walk down it, apparently quite calm, and disappear into the gallery. I told Alf Davies to man the gun and took the big miner up on to the bridge and down through the conning tower hatch. Well, I thought to myself, I suppose we're lucky to have any sort of a chance at all. After all, I had been expecting to try to blow myself and every one else into the next world. But I must say I did not relish the idea of trying to manoeuvre the submarine out through the underwater mouth of the cave under her own power with only three men on board who knew anything about the works, and unwilling men at that. Our only hope was that they were not all the heroic type.

I led the way for'ard to the magazine room. It was the hand-grenades I was after. I had the germ of an idea at the back of my mind. At that moment I don't think it was conscious. But it was sufficiently strong to direct me towards the grenades. We took up four each in our pockets, two rifles and a box of ammunition between us. We brought our haul out and laid it on the deck beside the gun. Then I looked at my watch. It was one-twenty-five. Another five minutes and first lunch would be over. Surely Logan ought to be back by now? But he had to get up to the top gallery. If the guard-room door were open he might have to bide his time.

At that moment there was a shout from the end of the dock. '*Wache*! Send those bastards down here to collect these cases.'

I poked my head round the conning tower. The same man

was standing in the tunnel leading down to the store-room. 'They'll come as soon as they've packed the stuff away up here,' I replied.

Then my heart sank. An officer had appeared, and I recognized him as the commander of U 21. He stopped and spoke to the man in the entrance to the store. The fellow pointed to the pile of cases on the deck and shrugged his shoulders. The commander nodded and came striding down the dockside. 'Get behind that gun,' I said. I dragged the rifles and the machine-gun out of sight. Then the two miners and myself crouched down, waiting.

The commander paused by the gangway. He looked up at the man mounting guard just for'ard of the conning tower, who had not moved a muscle, and then back at the gangway. I could just see his face between the mountings of the gun. He was puzzled by the position of the gangway. At length he stepped aboard and went aft. I picked up a rifle which I had loaded. I pushed forward the safety catch with my thumb. We were for it now. He would see the forge lying over the hatch. I left my hiding-place and moved quickly after him, my rifle ready. He bent over the forge. Then he began to shift it. I was about fifty feet from him. I put one knee to the deck and raised the rifle to my shoulder. 'You're covered,' I said in German. 'Put your hands behind your back and keep still.'

He swung round, and without a second's hesitation his hand went to his revolver. The choice was his. I pulled the trigger. The explosion in that confined space seemed deafening. His hand suddenly checked as it touched his holster, then his knees began to sag. I did not wait to see if he were dead. But as I raced for'ard I heard him slump to the deck. 'Man that gun,' I ordered.

Davies took his place beside the gun as I ran up. 'Hand-grenades,' I panted to the other miner. 'You look after No. 3 dock. I'll look after No. 5. We've got to block the gallery both sides.' He dived for the grenades, and despite his bulk had jumped on to the dock in a flash.

I picked up three grenades and followed him. I had dropped my rifle, but my revolver was still hanging round my neck by its lanyard. As we raced along the dock several men came running down the gallery. Two went past in the direction of No. 5 dock. But three more paused and came running to meet us. Fortunately they were ratings and therefore not armed. I fired, and though I had not aimed at any of them, they broke and ran. I was not accustomed to a revolver and I found the kick unexpectedly powerful.

Men had by now appeared in the entrance to the store-room. But they, too, were unarmed and drew back into the tunnel. We had almost reached the end of the dock now and I had drawn level with my miner. And at that moment I saw that one of the guards from No. 3 dock had appeared. But he held his rifle uncertainly, put out by our uniforms. 'Get back!' I yelled in German. 'Guard your own dock. It's mutiny.'

He did as I had ordered. But when we came to the gallery itself we found that he and two other guards were now standing across the gallery leading to No. 3 dock with their rifles at the ready. 'Okay,' I said to my companions. 'Out with the pins and let 'em have it.' I left him to look after the three guards whilst I took the gallery between our own and No. 5 dock. I could see men coming from other docks and out of the store-rooms farther along the gallery. I think we both tossed our grenades into the gallery at about the same time, for we were both running together with bullets singing past our ears and shrieking as they ricochetted off the walls.

Then came a terrific roar. And then another. The ground shook under our feet and a blast of hot air sent us both sprawling. My face hit the rocky surface of the dockside only half-protected by my upflung arm and I felt the blood warm in my nose. There was a horrible splitting noise as the rock began to crack. We clambered to our feet and staggered forward. And at the same moment there was a splitting and a rumbling behind us. I turned to see the whole roof of the gallery between our dock and No. 3 collapse. One moment I could see the white uniforms of the guards as they turned to run, and the next instant there was just a tumbled heap of rocks half-invisible in a cloud of dust.

My companion stumbled to his feet. There was a nasty cut across his left eye. The dust was beginning to clear now and I could see that the gallery leading to No. 3 dock was completely blocked. But I could not see what had happened to the right, between our own dock and No. 5, except that a whole lot of debris had spilled on to the floor of the gallery where it passed the end of our dock.

I ran back down the dock, a hand-grenade ready in my hand. The force of the explosion had broken most of the electric-light bulbs. But in the half-dark I was just able to see the white uniform of an officer, as he appeared up the tunnel from the store-room. The beam of a torch almost blinded me. 'What's happened?' he asked, mistaking me for one of the base guards. Then I suppose he saw the grenade in my hand, for he said: 'What are you up to?'

I had no alternative. I pulled the pin out, threw it into the tunnel in which he stood and ducked sideways. The bullet from his revolver sang past my head. A second later there was a flash and a great rumbling explosion. By one of those freak chances his torch remained alight and as it fell, it showed up for an instant the tunnel. The whole roof seemed to crumble. For an instant it actually hung suspended with small pieces of rock pouring from it. Then it came rumbling down and the whole scene went black.

I pulled the emergency torch that the guards always carried from my pocket and switched it on. The place was an absolute ruin. The whole of the end of the dock was just a pile of split and broken rock. Most of it was limestone, and it was then that I consciously realized why I had wanted the grenades. I had the limestone and there on the dock, behind me, was the oil storage tank and the smaller petrol tank. There was no chance of any one attacking us from this end for some time. I knew we had nothing to fear from the direction of No. 3 dock. Probably in all there were not more than twenty or thirty men working on docks 1, 2 and 3, including those in the munitions and fuel stores. They were trapped there, and the only means they had of rejoining the main body of the base was by swimming across the open ends of the docks. The danger would come from the direction of No. 5 dock. If only I had been able to block the ramp leading from the upper galleries! But I hadn't, and the whole personnel of the base would now be streaming into docks 5, 6 and 7. I listened. Between the intermittent sound of crumbling rock I could hear shouts and the murmur of voices coming from the open end of the dock. I clambered over the debris of rock and examined the fall between our own and No. 5 dock in the light of my torch. Where the gallery had been was solid rock from floor to ceiling. I reckoned that it would take them several hours to clear it sufficiently to attack us from this side, even using mobile drills to break down the large pieces of rock.

Having satisfied myself that we could not be taken in the rear, I scrambled back over the debris and rejoined the big miner. In an endeavour to wipe the blood from his eyes he had smeared his whole face with it. 'Come on!' I said. 'We've got to move the machine-gun up to the stern of the submarine.' My orders were entirely automatic. I had been over the whole thing so many times in my own mind that I knew exactly what to do. But I had lost all sense of reality. I had involuntarily slipped into the war mentality. When I had thrown the grenade at the stores officer he had been just a target, not a human being. It was the first time I had killed a man.

We ran back to the gangway and rejoined Davies and the other miner. They were both standing by the gun. Davies I told to remain with the gun. Briefly I explained the necessity of its being fired before we were overwhelmed. Then I and the big miner, whose name was Kevan, picked up the light machine-gun and carried it aft. The third miner, Trevors, followed with the magazines, a rifle and several grenades.

We rigged the gun up in the stern of the U-boat and stacked round it several cases of canned goods to act as a barricade. Then Trevors, who had been a machine-gunner in the last war, got down and fired a burst to make certain that the gun was in working order. It was. The clatter of it seemed to fill the cave. What is more, he hit his mark, which had been the top of the haulage gear buoy floating in the main cave. The bullets made a hollow sound as they struck the huge round cylinder and then ricochetted off to finish with a dull thwack against the sides of the cave.

As soon as I was certain that he could handle the gun satisfactorily, I took Kevan and ran back along the submarine to the conning tower. My aim was to get sufficient arms to ensure that we should be able to hold the end of the dock long enough for me to carry out my plan. It was the only chance—flimsy though it was—of our re-establishing contact with Logan and Maureen and of getting out of the base. There was no chance now of slipping out on the high tide and attempting to run the submarine through the undersea exit on her engines. As soon as we were out in the main cave we should be under the fire of the other submarines in the base and, before we had a chance to submerge, we should be sunk. True, that would probably achieve our object of blocking the undersea exit. But the plan I had in mind would achieve that and at the same time give us all a chance of escape.

Altogether we made four trips to the magazine of the submarine. The first thing we brought up was another light machine-gun, four magazines and some more hand-grenades. These we carried aft. Before going back for further arms, I made Trevors experiment with the changing of the magazines. It didn't take him long to find out how they worked and after seeing him fire a test burst from this gun, we returned to the submarine. Thereafter we brought up another light machine-gun, which we placed beside Davies at his post by the gun, four automatic rifles together with the necessary magazines and a further supply of grenades.

As we came up with the last load the soft chug-chug of the little diesel-engined tug could be heard. We raced aft, and at the same moment Trevors opened fire with his machine-gun. We had covered about half the distance when I saw a small dark object hurtle through the air. It dropped into the water just abaft the stern of U 21, and almost immediately a big column of water was thrown up and was followed by a muffled roar.

We flung ourselves down behind the packing cases and Kevan took over the spare machine-gun. I picked up an automatic rifle. The deck was very wet and Trevors was soaked. It was clear what they had tried to do. If they could cause a heavy fall of rock at the entrance to the dock they could trap us completely. Their difficulty was that they could not hit the entrance to the dock without exposing themselves to our fire. Nevertheless, the underwater explosion of the grenade they had thrown had apparently damaged the flood gates of the dock, for I could hear the water gurgling below us as it entered the dock. As far as I could tell the tide was about an hour beyond the high.

The engine of the tug sounded very close now. The boat was in fact just off the entrance to No. 5 dock and was only protected by the buttress of rock that separated the two docks. The tug's engines seemed suddenly to rev up. Trevors reached for a grenade. He had the pin out the instant the boat's nose showed beyond the buttress. I knelt on one knee and raised my automatic rifle, sighting it over the top of our protecting pile of packing cases. The boat, with its propeller threshing the water into a foam at its stern, seemed to shoot out from the cover of the buttress.

I sighted my rifle and pulled the trigger. It was like holding a pneumatic drill to one's shoulder as it pumped out a steady stream of bullets. I heard the clatter of Kevan's machine-gun at my side and sensed rather than saw Trevor's arm swing as he threw the grenade. The man at the wheel of the boat collapsed under our fire and another in the bows stopped dead in the act of throwing a grenade and crumpled up in the bottom of the boat. Almost immediately there was a terrific explosion and the boat seemed to split in half. It sank instantly, leaving a mass of wreckage, oil and three dead bodies floating on the surface of the water.

It was not a pleasant sight. Kevan said: 'Good for you, Steve.' But Trevors shook his head. 'Mine fell short,' he said. 'It was one of you two shooting that fellow in the bows that done it. He had the pin out when you hit him and the grenade exploded right in the bottom of the boat.'

At that moment we came under machine-gun fire from dock No. 7. But the shooting was wild, the reason being that the last explosion had put the remaining lights in our dock out. Shortly afterwards, however, they rigged up a searchlight. We then moved farther back into the dock. It was the only thing to do. They might risk casualties, but we daren't. We built a second barricade of packing cases, this time in a complete semi-circle across the deck, for we were being worried by the ricochet of bullets from the side of the cave. The trouble was that because the seven docks branched off fan-shape from the main cave, it was possible for the Germans operating from No. 7 to cover the mouth of our own dock.

I called up Davies to the shelter of our new barricade and we held a council of war. Then I explained my plan. 'It may work or it may not,' I said. 'We'll just have to risk it. Unless any of you have any other ideas?' But none of them had. We were trapped and it was only a matter of time before we would be overwhelmed. We were four against at least six hundred, and if we surrendered we should be shot. 'We can't hold this dock a minute if they float a submarine out before the tide falls,' I said. 'One shot from a six-inch gun at the mouth of this dock will trap us if it doesn't kill us. If they miss the tide, however, we may be able to hold out for as long as ten hours.'

'Whatever happens,' I went on, 'we've got to block the entrance to this base.' I then told them of the plan to attack a squadron of British capital ships which it was known would be for a time insufficiently screened by destroyers. I said: 'I suggest we proceed straight away with the demolition of the underwater entrance.'

To this they agreed. Even if they missed the tide I was afraid that under cover of fire from No. 7 dock they might try to block the entrance of our dock with grenades thrown from the collapsible rubber boats that the U-boats carried. I explained this and Trevors volunteered to go aft again and extinguish the light of the searchlight with machine-gun fire. But I said: 'Wait until we've fired this gun.'

3

Surprise

I left Davies to operate the gun and climbed up to the bridge of U 21. I switched on the U-boat's searchlight and swung it round, so that its brilliant beam was shining straight aft and illuminating the whole of the main cave. Towards the seaward end the roof sloped down until it disappeared below the level of the water, which showed black and oily in the bright light.

'Is it sighted correctly?' I asked.

'All correct,' replied Davies.

I braced myself against the rail of the bridge. 'Fire!' I said.

I saw Davies pull the trigger lanyard. Instantly there was a terrific explosion. I was practically thrown off my feet and I heard the hull plates of the U-boat grate most horribly on the rock of the empty dock. Almost simultaneously there was a blinding flash in the roof of the main cave, just where it disappeared below the water, and an explosion that seemed, in that confined space, to numb my whole body. A great wind of hot air struck my face and, in the light of the searchlight, I saw the whole far end of the cave collapse in a deep rumbling roar.

As a sight it was terrific. I had not fully realized the explosive power of a six-inch shell. The dock in which the U 21 lay was at least a hundred and fifty yards from the spot where the shell struck. Yet I could feel the whole of the rock round me tremble and vibrate, and quite large pieces of rock fell from the roof of our dock, making a hollow sound as they struck the submarine's deck. At least thirty yards of the main cave had collapsed. Huge masses of rock fell into the water, and as they fell a great wave rose in the basin. I yelled out to the others to hold tight. I don't think they heard, but they saw it coming—a great wall of water that surged down the main cave and swept up into the dock. It must have been a good ten feet high, for it swept into the empty dock almost at deck height. The submarine reared up on it like a horse as it suddenly floated. I had fallen flat on the bridge of the conning tower, and as the submarine lifted, I heard the rail strike the roof just above my head and the searchlight went out. Then the bows jarred violently against the end of the dock.

At any moment I expected to be crushed to death. But after bucking up and down for a moment, grating sickeningly against the sides of the dock, the submarine settled down again, this time afloat. Through my singing ears I heard the water running out through the damaged flood gates of the dock. I scrambled to my feet. The place was as dark as pitch and I could hear shouts and cries. 'Are you all right, Mr Craig?' someone called out from the direction of the gun.

'Yes,' I replied. 'Are you?' And without waiting for his reply I hurried down the conning tower ladder. I paused at the bottom in order to accustom my eyes to the dark. There was a faint luminosity at the end of the dock. Presumably not all the lights of the base had been extinguished by the explosion. Around me everything was black with darkness, but where the dock ran out into the main cave there was a half-circle of indefinite light. Against this I could just make out the dark bulk of the gun and figures moving about it.

I suddenly remembered my torch. I pulled it out of my pocket and switched it on. The faces of the three miners looked white as they faced the light. But they seemed all right. Fortunately the water had not swept over the deck, so that, though they were all soaked with the water that had slopped up between the submarine and the dock walls, the machine-gun, rifles and ammunition were still beside the gun.

Armed with automatic rifles we went aft. The forge was still in position over the after hatch, but the water had swept right over the stern of the submarine and our barricades of packing cases had been swept away. The deck seemed strewn with tins and lumps of rock, and the dockside, which was still awash, was dotted with packing cases.

One of the machine-guns had fetched up against the deck stanchions. We retrieved this. The other was missing. The magazines were where we had left them and we were able to retrieve one of the automatic rifles from the dockside. Hastily we rebuilt our barricade of packing cases. This was not an easy task as both gangways had been smashed to pieces and most of the cases had to be passed up from the dockside and dragged up the sloping sides of the submarine by rope.

However, ten minutes' work saw our barricade complete again. All the grenades appeared to have rolled overboard, so I paid another visit to the magazine of the submarine. It was whilst I was getting the grenades from their racks that I noticed the crew's escape apparatus. It was much the same as the Davis equipment used in British submarines and they were stacked in a large rack of their own. I picked up one of them. It had a face mask and a large air bag which strapped round the waist. A small cylinder of oxygen completed the equipment. It was in fact just what I required.

I hurried on deck with the grenades to find the main cave brilliantly lit. The submarine in No. 6 dock had switched on its searchlight. Then I understood the reason for the cries and shouts. On the black oily surface of the water that was still slopping about in the main cave bobbed three collapsible rubber boats, two of them floating upside down.

'They were just going to launch an attack when we fired that gun,' I said, nodding in the direction of the boats, as I put the grenades down on the deck behind the packing cases.

Kevan said: 'Ar, we'll be able to hawld this place faw sawm tame naw.'

'How do you mean?' I asked.

'They'll nawt be able to get the bawts awt naw. Dawn't ye feel us grainding on the bottom of the dawck?'

He was right. I had been too busy to notice it. Though the water had flooded the dock, the tide had receded sufficiently for the hull of the submarine to be just touching the bottom.

'Thank God for that!' I said. They had lost their chance. Our worst danger had been postponed. We had ten hours' grace so far as attack from another submarine went. Then and there I decided that, if the worst came to the worst and my own scheme failed, we would try to get our own boat out before the others and go down fighting rather than face a firing squad. It seemed easy to face death now that we were in action. I wondered what had happened to Logan.

Having completed our barricade, I left Davies and Trevors to hold the end of the dock and took Kevan down on to the dockside. The water had receded now. By the wall we found picks and shovels that had been used the previous day for erecting the derrick. We took these to the end of the dock, where the gallery had been blocked, and set to work to clear a space in the midst of the debris. We kept our automatic rifles handy in case the open end of the dock should be attacked.

Mostly we did the work with our hands, advancing steadily into the debris and piling the rocks behind us. It was a gigantic task and I was thankful that the work I had had to do in the fortnight I had been at the base had hardened my muscles. Even so, I found that Kevan, despite the fact that he had been unemployed for a considerable time, worked just about twice as fast as I was able to.

Half an hour passed and the basin I was trying to hollow out in the debris was beginning to take shape. We worked in silence and without pause. The constant stooping to throw out great lumps of limestone soon made my back ache abominably. We had climbed high on to the pile of fallen rock and were tossing the broken lumps out behind us so that the rim of the basin behind gradually rose. It was slow and hard work. Not only did my back and arms ache, but we were both constantly coughing with the rock dust.

At the end of half an hour, as though by common consent, we straightened our backs, and took a breather. I looked at my watch. It was just past three. I was standing now behind a huge circular rampart of rock. The roof, all jagged and looking very unsafe, was about ten feet above my head. On three sides of us the broken limestone was piled right to the roof. Only in the direction of the docks did the rock fall away, and here we were piling it up in order to make a kind of rock tank. This rampart had grown by now practically as tall as ourselves. I looked over it and along to the open end of the dock. The searchlight was still flooding the main cave and the light from it glistened on the wet walls of the dock and threw the conning tower of the submarine into black silhouette. The great dark shape of the boat seemed to fill the whole cave, and at the far end I could see our barricade of packing cases. I could see no sign of Davies and Trevors, however, for they lay in the shadow cast by the cases.

As I bent to resume my work, I saw Kevan standing tense at my side, listening. There was the sound of slipping rock, and then voices. It came from behind the fall that blocked the gallery between ourselves and No. 5 dock. Then came the unmistakable ring of metal on stone. 'They're trying to clear the fall,' said Kevan.

'How long will it take?' I asked.

He looked at the fall. The whole gallery had been blocked. 'Depends on the depth,' he said. 'I reckon it'll take them all of a good hour.'

'Good!' I said. 'By then we'll have finished this. Then we'll wait for them to come through. The draught will help.'

We resumed our work. But about ten minutes later the whole

place suddenly resounded to the clatter of machine-gun fire. It came from the open end of the dock. In an instant we were over the rampart of stone we had been piling up, had collected our automatic rifles and were running as hard as we could along the dockside.

There was a muffled explosion and a column of water shot up just abaft the stern of the submarine. We clambered on to the deck of the submarine and as I ran down it, I saw a figure half-rise from behind the barricade of packing cases and an instant later there was a loud roar and lumps of rock fell from the roof of the main cave into the water. At the same instant the searchlight was switched off.

We threw ourselves down behind the packing cases, our rifles ready. 'What's happened?' I panted.

'They had rigged up a raft,' replied Davies. 'There were several of them protected by packing cases. They had automatic rifles and one of them was flinging grenades. But Trevors got them with one of his grenades. Blew the whole raft apart.'

'Good work!' I said. 'Do you think you could hold them off for another half-hour, Trevors?' I asked.

There was no reply.

I put out my hand to where he lay behind his machine-gun. My hand touched his face. It was resting against one of the packing cases and it was warm and sticky. I screened my torch with my hands and switched it on. His muscular little body was crumpled up beside his gun, the back of his head resting on the protruding corner of a packing case. His blue unshaven jaw hung open, and his jacket was sodden with blood. A bullet had caught him in the throat.

I felt a sudden sickening sensation inside me. One out of four. There were only three of us now. Trevors had stood up in order to make sure of his aim. At the sacrifice of his own life he had demolished the raft. But there would be another raft and another. I said: 'We've got to get on with that job quickly. Can you finish off that basin, Kevan? It wants to be at least three feet deeper. I'll stay here with Davies and hold the fort.'

I heard him scramble to his feet. 'Give me a shout,' I said, 'when it's complete.' I gave him my torch and saw his big figure outlined against its light hurry back down the deck of the submarine.

Then Davies and I and the dead Trevors settled down to wait for the next attack. The searchlight had been switched on again and in its light I saw a German rating dive into the oily waters of the main cave and rescue a man who was injured and drowning. He was the sole survivor of the crew of the raft. Swimming steadily on his back and holding the injured man's head between his hands, the German disappeared into the neighbouring dock. Then the searchlight was switched off again. Three pools of light marked the entrances to docks 5, 6 and 7. Then one by one these were extinguished. To the left of our own dock everything was in complete darkness. To the right, however, docks 1, 2 and 3 still showed a faint glow of light.

Suddenly a voice shouted in German: 'Put those lights out over there.' The order was repeated several times. Then one by one the lights of these three docks were switched off. We were plunged into total darkness. It seemed to press down on us like a curtain. We could see nothing, not even the cases in front of us.

'They are going to try attacking in the dark,' whispered Davies.

'We'll just have to listen for them,' I said.

'Why wait for Kevan to deepen the basin?' he asked. 'Why not get on with your scheme right away?'

'It's no use doing it by halves,' I said. 'Once we get it going there's no possibility of feeding the fire.'

So we lay there in the dark and the minutes slipped slowly by. Gradually my ears accustomed themselves to all the various sounds in the docks. It was difficult to distinguish them, for they merged into each other to form a peculiar bustling murmuring sound. But occasionally I could pick out words of command and the sound of boots on rock, and from No. 5 dock came the persistent sound of tumbling rock as they worked to clear the fall and get through into our own dock.

It was an eerie business, lying there waiting for heaven knew what. I kept on mistaking the movement of the water for the sound of a raft being paddled towards us. I found myself praying desperately that Kevan would finish the work before the attack was launched. But I knew it must take him a full half-hour working on his own, and as I lay watching the luminous dial of my wrist-watch the minutes seemed to tick by incredibly slowly. A quarter of an hour passed by. Once I raised my rifle and was on the point of firing. But it was nothing. The darkness was absolutely impenetrable. Twenty minutes. Then we heard a new sound, a sound of hammering.

'They're making another raft,' whispered Davies.

At that moment my eyes were attracted by the flickering of a torch from the far end of our own dock. Kevan wanted me. 'I shan't be long,' I said to Davies, and screening a torch, which I had removed from Trevors, I hurried along the deck of the submarine. As soon as I could, I jumped down on to the dock and began to run.

Kevan met me by the oil tank. He said: 'They're almost through the fall.' I could hear the sound of shifting rocks quite clearly.

'Okay,' I said, 'let's pump the oil in.'

There was no time to see whether the basin in the limestone was sufficiently deep. We took hold of the oil tank and dragged it on its trolley to the edge of the debris. Then, while Kevan took the canvas pipe across the debris and laid it over the rampart of rocks so that the nozzle hung down into the basin, I ran back for the smaller petrol tank. Each tank was fitted with a hand pump, and Kevan was already pumping the oil into the basin by the time I had got the pipe of the petrol tank into position. In the light of my torch I could see the black crude oil pouring down amongst the rocks. At the same time I was uncomfortably aware of the sound of voices and falling rocks in the direction of No. 5 dock. At any moment I expected the Germans to break through.

I scrambled back to the petrol tank and began pumping, thankful to have my automatic rifle beside me. When the gauge told me I had half-emptied the tank, I went over to help Kevan. The oil tank was still nearly three-quarters full.

I found that Kevan had no need of my assistance, so I looked around and found a length of iron piping and some rags. I tied the rags round one end of the piping and then dipped them first in oil and then petrol. The resultant torch I put down on top of the oil tank. By this time the sound of the Germans coming through the fall was becoming much louder, until by the murmur of their voices I was quite certain that they had broached it.

Kevan straightened his back. The oil tank was empty. I played my torch over the rampart of rock. It seemed to be holding the oil quite satisfactorily. Then, quite distinctly, I heard an exclamation in German. Evidently they had seen the light. Kevan had started the pump of the petrol tank. I could hear the liquid pouring out into the basin. I raised my automatic rifle to cover the spot where the Germans would emerge.

At that moment there was a burst of machine-gun fire from the open end of the dock. I glanced round. Was it another attack? There was no light at all. After the one burst there was silence. Perhaps Davies had made a mistake? Then, faintly, came the sound of Davies's voice speaking. I could not hear what he said, but I was convinced he was speaking to the Germans in the next dock. 'Hurry!' I said to Kevan.

'Nearly finished,' he replied.

Then echoing down the dock came Davies's voice. 'Mr Craig! Mr Craig!' There was a note of urgency in it.

I took the matches from my pocket and thrust them into

Kevan's hand. 'Light the torch and throw it into the basin as soon as you're ready,' I said. 'But for God's sake don't let them get through first.'

'Ar, I'll see to it.' He took the matches, never pausing in his pumping, and I ran down the dock as hard as I could.

'Mr Craig!' Davies's voice again. I clambered on to the deck of the submarine. My shoes rang hollow on the steel plates. At last I put out my torch and felt my way forward to the packing cases. 'What is it?' I asked as I threw myself down beside Davies.

'They've got Miss Weston and your friend Logan.'

'Well?'

'They say they've got them bound and are going to use them as a shield for a machine-gunner unless we surrender. I asked them to wait so that I could consult you.'

At that moment the searchlight of the submarine in the next dock was switched on. Then I understood. Floating just off the entrance to No. 5 dock was a raft, and strapped to it in a kneeling position were Maureen Weston and Big Logan. They were kneeling side by side, and between them poked the muzzle of a machine-gun. It was quite impossible for us to fire at the gunner behind without hitting them. I saw Big Logan's huge body rigid with the effort of trying to tear himself clear of his bonds. The sweat was glistening on his broad forehead and his long brown hair was lank. Maureen looked quite fresh, but the position in which she was held was obviously most uncomfortable. The raft was slowly moving towards us, propelled, I imagine, by at least two ratings swimming in the rear.

'Will you surrender? Or will you risk the lives of your friends?' I recognized the voice as that of Commodore Thepe.

'What are the conditions?' I asked to gain time.

'There will be no conditions,' was the sharp reply.

'Don't be a bloody fool,' said Logan. 'They're going to shoot you.' I saw an arm move from behind him and his body jerked at the sudden pain of a jab from a bayonet.

'You stick to your guns, Walter,' Maureen said. 'Don't worry about us. We'll be shot anyway.'

At that moment I heard the sound of a shot from the dock behind me. I turned to see the distant figure of Kevan stagger, the torch I had left with him blazing in his hand. In the light of it I could just see the figure of a German high up on the rocks above the basin. Then Kevan's arm swung and the blazing torch sailed in a perfect arc into the rock basin. There was an instantaneous flash that lit up the whole dock as the petrol lying on top of the crude oil ignited. Then the whole of the end of the dock seemed suddenly ablaze. What happened to the Germans coming through over the fall from No. 5 dock I cannot imagine. The heat must have been terrific, and the flames were immediately drawn through the gap by the draught. The sound of the flames came down the dock like the roar of a mighty wind. And against their intense light I could see the big ungainly figure of Kevan come stumbling down the dockside, his shadow flickering along the wall of the dock in front of him.

And at that moment the machine-gunner on the raft opened fire on us. I told Davies to make a dash for it. He hesitated an instant, crouching behind the packing cases. Then he darted out and ran as hard as he could down the deck of the submarine. I heard his boots ringing on the deck plates as I opened fire with our own machine-gun. I aimed to the side of the raft, well clear of Maureen and Logan, but it was sufficient to keep the gunner's attention from Davies long enough for him to get into the dock, out of the line of fire.

Almost consciously I forced myself not to think of the possi-bilities I faced. I had to get for'ard to the conning tower. I bunched my legs up under me and then jumped to my feet and started running as hard as I could down the deck. The light of the flames made it quite easy to see my way without a torch. I remember consciously thinking how little time had passed, for, as I started to run, I saw Kevan's figure still running towards us along the dockside.

Bullets began to whistle to the left of me and I was uncomfortably aware of the persistent clatter of the machine-gun behind me. The gunner had been prepared for my dash and he had swung his gun on me almost before I had broken cover.

I learned later from Maureen that I owed my life at this moment to Logan. As I rose from behind the packing cases he made a superhuman effort to shift himself sufficiently to upset the aim of the gun. He just managed to touch the gun with his elbow and so shift it out of alignment. This occurred, I suppose, just as the gunner swung his gun towards me, for I had not run more than a few yards when I received what felt like a violent kick in the left arm, accompanied immediately by a sharp pain. After that the bullets went wide, and in a few seconds I passed out of the gunner's line of sight.

I saw Kevan struggling on to the deck of the submarine. He seemed unable to use his right arm, and by the dancing light of the flames I could see the sweat glistening on his face. Davies was standing irresolute at the foot of the conning tower. 'Get inside,' I yelled. He began to swarm up the ladder to the bridge. Kevan reached it just before I did. I followed him up, but when I tried to grasp the rails of the ladder I cried out with the sudden pain in my left arm. The forearm was broken just above the wrist and was bleeding fast.

With my right arm I pulled myself up the ladder. From the bridge of the conning tower I took one brief glance round. In the lurid light, I could just make out a corner of the raft as it slowly approached the end of the dock. At the other end, our improvised tank of oil and petrol was burning furiously. Then I tumbled down the conning tower hatch and closed it after me, fastening it on the inside.

Coming down from the conning tower, I found Davies bandaging Kevan's shoulder. There was a nasty wound just near the arm joint. I ran quicky aft to the store-room bulkhead. I dragged the bulkhead back. The imprisoned Germans were sitting on the packing cases. They sprang up as the door opcned. I covered them with my revolver. 'Put your hands above your heads,' I said in German. I backed down the gangway, keeping them covered. 'Follow me!' I backed as far as the engine-room hatch. 'Open that!' I ordered the officer.

He turned back the lever and pulled the hatch open. 'Now get down there—all of you,' I ordered. I saw the officer hesitate, weighing up his chances. '*Wache!*' I called. Then I said: 'Get down there.' My call for the guard seemed to settle him, for he went through the hatch and the others followed him. I closed it and fastened it. Then I went back into the store-room. As I climbed the ladder to the hatch I heard the sound of boots moving stealthily along the deck above my head. I fastened the hatch. Then I went for'ard to see about the hatch through which the munitions had been lowered. By the time I had climbed up and fastened this I was feeling pretty faint. Walking back along the gangway, I found myself following a trail of my own blood.

I arrived back in the control room to find Kevan just easing his shoulder into his jacket. 'Better?' I asked. Davies turned at the sound of my voice and then exclaimed: 'Good God in heaven, Mr Craig! Whatever is the matter with you?'

I pointed to my left arm. 'Do you think you can manage a tourniquet?'

'Why, yes, indeed.'

He took my coat off, rolled my sleeve back and then with a strip of material torn from his shirt, he bound my arm just above the elbow. 'You'll want a splint too,' he said, and broke a heavy chart ruler in half. I then spent a most painful five minutes. The force of the bullet had pushed the bone out of place so that splinters were showing through the mess of blood and broken skin. I think I passed out twice whilst Davies was resetting it. 'Lucky it is you are with a miner, Mr Craig,' Davies said, as he bandaged it into place against the splints. 'It's not every one that knows how to set a broken limb properly, is it now?'

I agreed that it wasn't, and sat down on the chart table, feeling rather uncertain of my legs. 'What do we do now?' asked Davies.

'Wait. Just wait,' I said. 'And pray that they don't get into the submarine before the fire has got properly to work on the limestone.'

We stayed in the control room for some time, listening to the sound of footsteps overhead. I could imagine the puzzlement of the Germans. What would they think? One minute we are holding the dock, and the next a huge fire is blazing and we have disappeared inside the submarine. I could imagine the raft plying to and fro between our dock and No. 5 bringing more and more men on to the scene. What would they do about the fire? Would they try to put it out? Even if they had been able to get their fire-fighting equipment into our dock, they hadn't a hope of extinguishing it.

'Let's examine the oxygen supply,' I said. I was feeling a little better now. But the submarine was getting very hot. I could imagine the terrific heat of that fire reddening the bow plates. If we were forced to stay in the submarine any length of time it would become a death trap—a positive oven.

We found the oxygen supply equipment. Davies seemed to know how it worked. It looked very complicated to me. Footsteps kept running backwards and forwards over our heads. It was very eerie in that submarine. All movements on deck came to us as hollow sounds. Very faintly we could hear the sound of voices. The air was already beginning to get stale. I knew we could not have already used up the available air, so I presumed that some of the CO_2 given off by the fire in the limestone basin was beginning to seep into the submarine. The hatches were only fully airtight when subjected to pressure from water outside. Davies switched on the oxygen supply.

I went along the gangway and through the magazine to the

spot where I had seen the escape apparatus. From the rack I took five sets of equipment. They consisted of a mask, which clipped over the head and covered the nose and mouth, an air bag which was strapped round the body and a small cylinder of oxygen. To my great relief I discovered that the oxygen cylinders were filled.

As I joined the others I heard a muffled hissing noise coming from the direction of the conning tower. We went into the control room. It was louder there and coming from the hatch. 'Sounds like an oxy-acetylene cutter,' said Davies.

'I'm afraid so,' I said. 'Better stand by to repel boarders.' We found a revolver for Kevan. Davies was the only one capable of using an automatic rifle. As we stood staring up at the conning tower hatch we saw the metal of it suddenly redden at one point. It glowed like a cigarette in the half-darkness, then broadened and whitened. An instant later molten metal was dripping down at our feet and the flame of the cutter had appeared.

We watched the brilliant white flame slowly cutting through the metal. There was a sort of horrible fascination about it. It was a race between the cutter and the gas given off by the fire. Or had the fire been put out? I did not think so for the submarine was so hot. But my mind was so hazy that I could not be certain of anything. Anyway, I was so exhausted that it didn't seem to matter one way or the other.

A large part of the hatch now showed a dull red. The white line of cut metal grew until it showed as a definite segment of a circle. Very slowly I could see the cutting flame moving through the metal. The sound of it was now much louder. Soon the segment had grown to a semi-circle. 'What do we do—fight or surrender?' asked Kevan.

'We'd better take a vote on it,' I said. I was feeling very depressed. My mind kept groping over the formula—$CaCO_3 = CaO + CO_2$. Surely that was right? Or had I made a mistake? Then suddenly I saw that the cutting flame was no longer

201

moving. 'He's stopped,' I said. We watched. The whiteness of the metal where it had been cut was dimming. It was reddening, and the hatch cover as a whole was becoming black again. Gradually the hiss of the oxy-acetylene blower dwindled until it had stopped altogether.

'Thank God!' I breathed. 'Listen!' Not a sound. I walked down the length of the submarine and back again. There was not a sound from the deck overhead. When I rejoined the others in the control room I said: 'Davies—you and I will go out and bring in Logan and Miss Weston.'

Kevan helped us into the escape apparatus. We blew the air bags up and switched on the oxygen. Then, wearing a pair of gloves, Davies unfastened the hatch and threw it back. I carried two spare oxygen equipments. We clambered out, breathing through our masks. The fire was still roaring, the flames flickering redly on the rock walls of the dock. Quickly we slammed the hatch back to conserve the pure air in the submarine. As we did so the body of the acetylene cutter rolled face upwards. It was a horrible sight. He had collapsed on to the flame of the blower and his face was burned out of all recognition.

The deck of the submarine presented a most amazing sight. There must have been at least twenty Germans lying huddled where they had collapsed. We hurried to the stern where we found two collapsible rubber boats moored. In one there was a German seated at the oars. He was looking dazed, but was not properly unconscious. But even as we climbed into the other boat, which was empty, he collapsed.

I cast off and Davies rowed quickly round to dock No. 5. Here the sight was even more amazing. The whole dock seemed strewn with the bodies of German sailors. It was like rowing in some fantastic crypt filled with the dead. I looked at Davies, pulling steadily on the oars, his face obscured by the awful futurist mask. So one might depict a modern Charon rowing a new-comer to Hades across the river Styx.

We moored to the flood gates of No. 5 dock and Davies scrambled up on to the dockside. I remained in the boat. In a very short while he returned, dragging Big Logan's unconscious body. I thought I should never be able to get him into the boat safely. But, rocking precariously, I lowered it into the bottom of the boat. Maureen's slight figure was easier to handle. Within less than three minutes of landing we were rowing back to No. 4 dock. Whilst Davies rowed, I fitted the escape apparatus first on to Logan and then on to Maureen. Then I untied their remaining bonds, not an easy procedure since I could use only one hand. Almost as soon as he began to breathe the oxygenized air, Logan showed signs of life. The first thing he did when he recovered consciousness was to try to tear the mask from his face. This I managed to prevent him from doing, and by the time we had reached our own dock, he had recovered sufficiently to lift himself on to the submarine. By that time Maureen had also recovered consciousness, but she needed assistance in climbing up on to the deck of the submarine.

Back in the interior of the submarine, we removed their masks and our own. Kevan had plugged the circular cut in the conning tower hatch, and the oxygenized air in the submarine was good to breathe after the mask, which was not at all comfortable. The place was getting very hot indeed, however, and I did not think we should be able to stay there much longer. Kevan had also found a flask of brandy. He passed it first to Maureen. Then on to Logan and so to myself.

Soon after the brandy Maureen lost her dazed look and asked conventionally where she was. I explained what had happened, and she giggled a little uncertainly. 'I never thought I should live to be rescued by you, Walter,' she said. I didn't know quite how to take this, so remained silent. Her dark hair was hanging over her eyes, and flushed with newly regained consciousness, she looked startingly provocative. I saw Logan watching her.

I said: 'I'm afraid you've had rather an unpleasant time.'

But she shook her head. 'No, it wasn't too bad. As soon as Dan here saw the fire he told me what you were up to. You put us to sleep quite comfortably, didn't he?' She turned to Logan.

'Is your name Dan?' I asked.

Logan grinned. 'Yes, they even gave me a Christian name,' he said. 'Where's Trevors?' he added.

'Dead,' I said.

There was a long silence.

By this time every one seemed sufficiently recovered, so I suggested that we started out for the back exit of the base. We put on our oxygen apparatus and each of us took a spare. Also we took one of the submarine's oxygen cylinders, just in case. We had no idea how long our apparatus would keep us going. Then I sent Kevan aft to place a packing case or something fairly heavy over the engine-room hatch and unfasten it. I did not want the men down there to be trapped in this oven.

When we tied up at No. 5 dock and clambered up on to the dockside I was once again conscious of the eeriness of the place. There were men everywhere, but not a soul stirred. It was like a place of the dead. And we five masked figures looked like five horrible ghouls picking our way amongst the dead. The Germans seemed to have been struck down without warning. One still knelt before a piece of wood he had been sawing, kept upright by the saw. It was difficult to believe that they were only unconscious as yet, not dead.

At the end of the dock we found one of the mobile drills. They had been using it to get through the fall that blocked the gallery into our own dock. We then found two more cylinders of oxygen and several picks and placed them on top of the drill. We passed the ends of docks 6 and 7 and then dragged the drill up to the upper galleries. On the ramp and in the galleries we had to skirt unconscious bodies and sometimes they lay so thick that we had to move them in order to get the drill through.

At last we arrived at the guard-room and the cells we knew

so well. Logan and Davies, who were armed with automatic rifles, went in front. They threw open the door, their rifles raised in case the gas had not penetrated the closed door. But the guard-room was empty. Davies went straight across to the other side where a rack of rifles stood. He pushed it sideways. A whole section of the cemented wall slid back on rollers to reveal a black cavity in the rock behind.

We hesitated, each looking questioningly from one to the other. Were we to risk everything in a desperate attempt to get through the falls in the mine? That meant blowing up the guard-room and imprisoning ourselves in the mine, for it was impossible to say how long the fire would last and once the men in the base regained consciousness they could come after us in order to prevent us making contact with the outside world. I remembered what Logan had said about falls in tin mines. It seemed pretty hopeless.

'Isn't there some sort of a lookout?' Maureen's voice was muffled by her mask.

'Yes,' I replied, 'but it's like a periscope—just a piece of steel piping thrust through the rock. We'd never get through.'

'Ventilation?'

I shook my head. 'What do you say, Logan?'

'This is our only chance,' was his reply.

'I agree,' I said. 'First, we need some food. And keep that door shut. We don't want to lose any good air there is in the mine.'

Davies pushed the section of wall back across the opening and he and Kevan remained in the guard-room, whilst Logan, Maureen and I went in search of food. In the nearest kitchen we found two of the cooks sprawled across the table and another had burned himself on the stove and slipped to the floor in front of it. We collected enough provisions for a week in a big packing case and a large can of water and dragged them along to the guard-room. We loaded them on to the drill trolley, and after providing ourselves with torches, some spare batteries, an automatic rifle each and magazines, together with several grenades, we went through into the mine.

I think we all felt somewhat chilled at leaving the lighted guard-room for this dark damp tunnel. It was like stepping straight from the warmth and comfort of civilization into some aged vault. To me it was like walking into one's grave, for I was not hopeful of our being able to break through the falls. There were only two of us properly able-bodied, and I was afraid that lack of ventilation would kill us long before our food gave out.

As soon as the section of the guard-room wall had been pushed back behind us we took off our masks. The air smelt damp and stale. By the light of a torch we walked steadily along the gallery, the drill trolley, now badly overloaded, jolting on the uneven floor. After we had gone about two hundred yards we came to a fall. This was the one that Maureen and her companions had worked their way through. She pointed to something. It was a piece of wire that led to one of the larger rocks. Evidently that was what had given the alarm. The gap they had made was not large and it proved quite impossible to get the trolley through. We debated whether to try to widen it or not. I was all for leaving the trolley. I had suddenly remembered that its engine would pollute the air. Anyway, it could be brought along later. The others agreed to this, so we unloaded it and passed all the various articles which we had loaded on to it through the narrow gap in the fall. It was a fearful struggle, and by the time everything we wanted had been transferred I felt completely exhausted. What little I had done had caused my arm to start bleeding again and I was conscious of the warm blood trickling down the splints on to my hand.

As soon as everything had been transferred to the farther side of the fall, I asked Davies if he would go back and demolish the guard-room. 'A few grenades will do the trick,' I said. 'But see that you leave yourself time to get clear. And keep the door into the mine as near shut as possible and hold your breath whilst you're in the guard-room.'

We wished him good luck and he climbed back through the fall. Gradually the sound of his footsteps died away. Then faintly we heard the door to the guard-room being slid back. Silence for a moment. Then the faint rumble of the door sliding to again and the sound of footsteps running towards us down the mine gallery. We braced ourselves for the explosion. It came a few seconds later, a terrific muffled roar that shook the rock in which the gallery was cut and seemed to rumble through our very bodies. It was not one explosion, but several very close together, and the roar of them and the crash of falling rock was continuous. Pieces of rock fell from the roof of the gallery round us and I felt the fall shift slightly.

Gradually silence descended on us again. We listened. Not a sound. We called out, but Davies did not answer. 'I'll go back for him,' said Logan.

'No, I will,' I said. I felt sick for fear I had sent the man to his death.

But before I could move Logan was already scrambling over the rocks of the fall. He had to shift great lumps of dislodged rock before he could get through the gap. Again we waited. Two or three minutes later we heard him coming back up the gallery. 'It's all right,' he called from the other side of the fall. 'He got laid out by a lump of rock.'

I felt greatly relieved. And shortly afterwards Davies himself climbed back through the gap in the fall. He had a nasty scalp wound, but otherwise seemed all right. 'The force of it knocked me over,' he said. 'Then a bloody great rock hit me on the side of the head.'

'I went back and had a look at the damage,' Logan said as he climbed through. 'The gallery is completely blocked some yards from the entrance to the guard-room.'

We had burned our boats. I think we all had that sinking

feeling. There was no going back. Whatever falls lay ahead, we just had to get through them. Each carrying as much as he could, we went on along the gallery. It sloped gradually upward and bore to the left. There were the remains of sleepers and here and there old lengths of rail on the floor of the gallery. Suddenly it broadened out and we found ourselves emerging from the farthest right of three branches off a main gallery. Logan, who was leading, glanced back at Davies. 'The main gallery,' said the Welshman. 'The other branches are no use whatever. They end in falls, and if you worked through them you'd most likely find yourself back with the submarines.'

So we pushed on up the main gallery. But we had not gone more than a hundred yards or so before we found the gallery completely blocked with rock. 'This is the fall they made yesterday,' said Davies.

'Looks pretty hopeless,' said Maureen rather dully.

'Depends how deep it goes,' was Davies's reply.

We put our things down and set to work immediately. Maureen tried to get Kevan and myself to rest. But I knew the value of time and though we could each use only one arm we were better than nothing.

Davies wielded a pick and the rest of us attacked the fall with our bare hands, pulling the loosened rocks down and piling them up behind us. When we started on it the time was just on four. But after that time had no meaning for me. It was dust and rocks and straining and heaving and sweating. Pain, too, for the exertion brought the blood pumping into my wound. Time went on and I really had no idea what progress we were making. I was just automatically pushing behind me rocks that were thrust at me from above. We took it in turns to rest. Sometimes we had water, sometimes some food, and days seemed to pass.

Nothing seemed real except my intense longing to rest. As in a dream I heard Logan say: 'Listen!' I listened, but I could hear nothing but the pumping of the blood against my ear drums.

But still as in a dream I saw the others getting wildly excited and setting to work furiously on the fall again. Once more I began automatically shifting the rocks that were thrust at me. Then I heard faint picking sounds beyond the fall and later I remember Maureen saying: 'It's all right, Walter, they're coming for us.'

I think it was then that I passed out, and I remember nothing until I woke to the lovely cold feel of fresh night air on my face. I had not felt fresh air for a fortnight. I breathed it in— sweet cool stuff smelling of grass and little rock plants. And then I opened my eyes and saw stars and a great round moon floating high in the velvet night. I closed my eyes again and slept.

The following is the report of Captain Marchant, which was forwarded to the War Office by the commanding officer at Trereen:

I proceeded to Pendeen with two companies, arriving there at 22.10 hours. Detective-inspector Fuller was awaiting my arrival at the inn, together with an officer of the Intelligence. The latter informed me that the Wheal Garth mine was believed to be occupied and to have some connection with U-boats. A woman reporter and three miners had failed to return from the mine after a visit the previous day.

There were three possible exits to the mine. I detailed a section to guard each of these exits. The fourth section I detailed to watch the cliffs above the mine. Lieutenant Myers took charge of these operations and each section was allotted a local miner as a guide.

With 'B' company I proceeded to the most recent shaft of the mine, which had been opened up by a rescue party. Detective-inspector Fuller informed me that he had had plant brought over from Wheal Geevor and that thirty miners were working in relays to clear the fall.

We then proceeded down the shaft by rope ladder and through several galleries to the fall. It was then 23.30 hours. At 2.20 hours sounds were heard from the other side of the fall. A way was cleared through and the woman reporter and two of the three miners who had gone down with her were discovered. With them were two men—Craig and Logan—who had disappeared after the landing of a U-boat commander near Cadgwith recently. They reported a complete submarine base with seven docks and accommodation for more than six hundred men. They had fought their way out largely by the ingenious method of causing a fire in a limestone fall and so immobilizing the base with CO_2. They had blocked the gallery behind them.

We proceeded to this fall, and by 5.40 hours had cleared a passage into the base. The gas had cleared and many of the Germans had regained consciousness. But they put up a weak resistance. By 6.50 hours we were in control of the whole base.

Our casualties were two dead—Sgt Welter and Pte Gates—and three wounded—Ptes Morgan, Chapman and Regal. The enemy lost four dead and six wounded in action against us. There were also a further forty-six dead by asphyxiation or by other means. Many were seriously ill as a result of the effects of the gas. A fall in the main gallery by the docks prevented those who resisted from getting at the munition stores and blowing up the whole base. One submarine was, however, destroyed by explosives.

Altogether five ocean-going U-boats have been captured intact and one destroyed, as mentioned above. Also one submarine store ship and a large quantity of war material fell into our hands. Prisoners taken totalled five hundred and sixty-five.

Signed,
MARCHANT.

Following a report by the intelligence officer to M.I.5 the proposed action against Kiel was postponed, it being feared that information concerning this plan might have been transmitted to Germany by a submarine.

After the capture of the base the area of sea immediately off the entrance was closely mined and a phosphorescent float moored in the usual position. By this means four more U-boats were destroyed.

THE END

THE HISTORY OF VINTAGE

The famous American publisher Alfred A. Knopf (1892–1984) founded Vintage Books in the United States in 1954 as a paperback home for the authors published by his company. Vintage was launched in the United Kingdom in 1990 and works independently from the American imprint although both are part of the international publishing group, Random House.

Vintage in the United Kingdom was initially created to publish paperback editions of books bought by the prestigious literary hardback imprints in the Random House Group such as Jonathan Cape, Chatto & Windus, Hutchinson and later William Heinemann, Secker & Warburg and The Harvill Press. There are many Booker and Nobel Prize-winning authors on the Vintage list and the imprint publishes a huge variety of fiction and non-fiction. Over the years Vintage has expanded and the list now includes great authors of the past – who are published under the Vintage Classics imprint – as well as many of the most influential authors of the present. In 2012 Vintage Children's Classics was launched to include the much-loved authors of our youth.

For a full list of the books Vintage publishes, please visit our website www.vintage-books.co.uk

For book details and other information about the classic authors we publish, please visit the Vintage Classics website www.vintage-classics.info

JUL 2013

www.vintage-classics.info

Visit www.worldofstories.co.uk for all your
favourite children's classics